SPLIT IMAGE

ANNA BLACK

DELPHINE PUBLICATIONS
ATLANTA

SPLIT IMAGE

Delphine Publications focuses on bringing a reality check to the genre urban literature. All stories are a work of fiction from the authors and are not meant to depict, portray, or represent any particular person.

Names, characters, places, and incidents are either the product of the author's imagination or are used fictitiously, and any resemblances to an actual person living or dead are entirely coincidental.

ISBN 13 - 978-0-9846923-8-5

Published by Delphine Publications
www.DelphinePublications.com

Printed in the United States of America

Acknowledgements

To the One and only true God of Israel. My Savior, my Source, my Lord. Through Christ all things are possible, so I thank Him. My family and friends, nothing but thanks to you for your constant support. To my proof readers Deccie and Ieshia, a huge thanks because you ladies rock. My publisher Delphine and to all the contributor's to my projects; thank you. A special thanks to Alanna for doing her editing thing, Davida for doing her cover thing and Nakia for doing her typesetting thing.

To God be the glory for my gift of writing. It has nothing to do with me, it is all Him and I thank Him. To have a creative mind is a gift and I truly thank Him.

Happy reading and always remember to;
Be You,
Do You,
Love You!

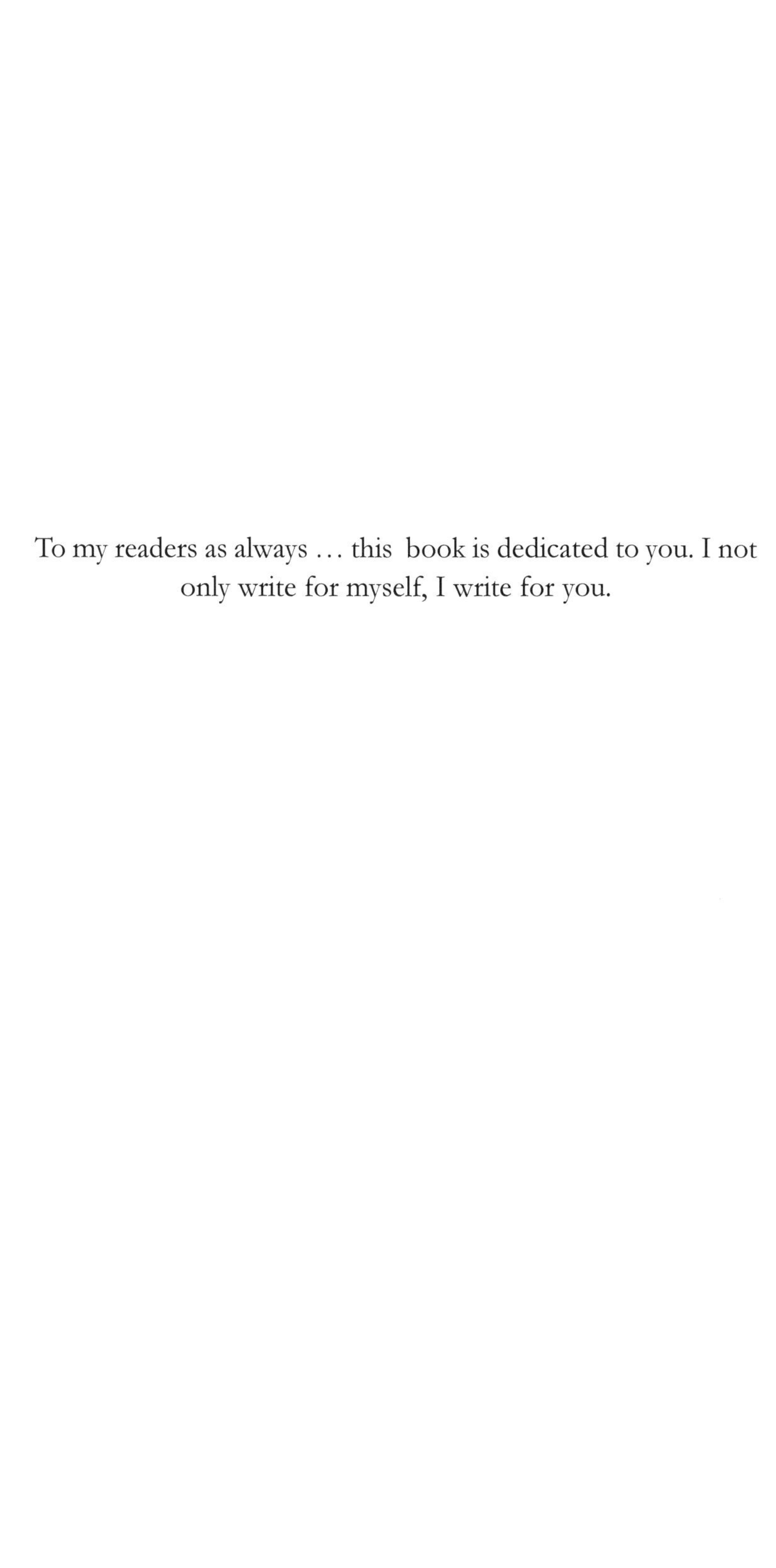

To my readers as always … this book is dedicated to you. I not only write for myself, I write for you.

SPLIT IMAGE

Chapter One

THAT SUNDAY morning was like most Sunday mornings in New Baptist Missionary Church. The congregation was on their feet praising God and enjoying Julia's two younger sisters, Jessica and Jada, sing "Lord, You've Been so Faithful." Julia swayed from side to side with her fan in her hand, and she smiled at her daddy sitting in his chair in the pulpit rocking his head and patting his feet. The service had come to an end, but after his message of God's faithfulness, he called for her two younger sisters to sing that selection before he gave the benediction.

Julia smiled at her younger sisters while they sang and thought back to when she was younger, when she and her twin sister Juliana used to sing side by side in her daddy's church and how she was always so afraid to take the first verse of the song, but Juliana didn't mind one bit and would have taken over the entire song if she had to. Julia watched Jessica and Jada and wished she could have just one more chance to sing a song with Juliana in her daddy's church again. She looked up to the ceiling and asked God another time to grant that request for her.

After the song was over, her daddy got up and went back to the podium and some people were still standing on their feet. "Ain't he all right?" her daddy sang, and the church said, "Amen." "God is faithful . . . God is always faithful . . . God is faithful when we are not faithful, church . . . So every time you say . . . God, why me? . . . or, God, how come? . . . just remind yourself how faithful God is," he sang in his southern minister tone, and the congregation continued to praise. He gave it a moment and allowed the church to give praise, and then he began to close. "Just remember to be faithful to Him and continue to have faith. As sure as He allowed that situation to come upon you, He is sure to bring you out, because God is faithful.

"Everyone, please stand to your feet," he said, and then he gave the benediction and made his way to the front doors to shake hands with the members as he did on all Sundays.

Julia and her sisters did what they normally did after the first service. They went through the aisles and put the Bibles that were left on the seat of the pews into the pockets on the back and picked up any visible paper so they could run the vacuum to get the church ready for the second service. They had two services every Sunday, one at 8 A.M. and the other at 1:00 p.m., and they always tried to end in time to clean and have lunch and make it back to start the next service.

That Sunday, Julia wanted to skip second service because Juliana was so heavy on her mind and she was anxious to get home to talk to her, but her daddy always had a saying about skipping church that rang in her ears and that was "Would you like it if God skipped you?" She knew that skipping church unless you were deathly ill was unacceptable in their house.

There wasn't much of an answer a Valentine could give for skipping Bible Study, choir rehearsal, revival, or any program that went on at their daddy's church, that's why she had some of her daddy's sermons memorized because he'd give the same message again from time to time.

She knew she was going to have to explain why she missed second service, but she had a funny feeling in her stomach and something was telling her she had to call her sister, so she followed her inner voice and went home. When she called, of course, they spent the first five minutes with Juliana reassuring her that everything was fine and after that, Julia asked her the same question she'd asked her every conversation that they had. She prayed to God each time to allow her sister to give her a different answer, but like before, she didn't.

"So when are you coming home?" Julia asked her sister.

"Girl, please, you know that is not going to happen. Daddy would spray me with holy water if I stepped on the lawn," she said, and they laughed.

"Yeah, you are right about that, that's for sure," Julia agreed.

"Hey, why don't you come out here to L.A.? It'll be a blast to have you," Juliana said.

"Jules, come on now—me in L.A.? That is funnier than Daddy hosing you down with holy water."

"No, it isn't. We can go shopping and hang out, and I can take you to the studio, and you can do a duet with me. Oh my God, Lia, that would be so great. Miles can write something special for us. Come on, it'll be fun."

"Miles? Who is Miles?" she asked, because all her sister ever talked about was some dude named Reg that she was going to someday marry.

"Well, Miles is this song writer that I'm kinda seeing, but you know how that goes," she said taking a sip of her drink.

"No way, Jules, you got more than one boyfriend?" her sister asked in amazement and in her Southern girl accent. They were country girls from a little town outside of Savannah, Georgia, and they were brought up Southern Baptist and boys were the one thing they really never had too much experience with because everybody respected their daddy. He was the pastor of the local church that mostly everyone in her town attended, and they knew the Valentine girls were off limits. Even Juliana was a virgin until she moved to New York.

"Girl, things are different in Cali than they are in Georgia, and here, there is no such thing as sin," Juliana said smiling and happy to be away from the small-minded, small world surroundings she grew up in. She was always the fast and ambitious sister of the five of them and swore she'd get out of that town as soon as she was of age. She saved every dime she had and as soon as she turned eighteen she left. She went to New York first and did a few auditions and landed a few roles in plays and before long she was in L.A. doing what she knew she was born to do and that was sing.

"Well, I beg to differ; the devil is all over and sin is everywhere," Julia protested.

"Look, Lia, I know and I don't need any sermons. I had enough of those in my days—that's for sure," she said walking into her massive closet. Her estate was larger than any home in her small town. Not even the senator of Georgia lived like she lived, and she hated her family didn't want any part of it. "Now, come on, I'll get you a first-class ticket, and you can come spend some time out here with me. It's been so many years since we've seen each other, and I miss you, sis," she pleaded.

"I know, Jules, I miss you too, and it's getting harder to keep this away from Daddy. Every time I mention your name he just gets, I don't know—," she said shaking her head.

"Well, Daddy is Daddy, and if Momma was here today, she'd tell him how wrong he is. He stands there in front of his congregation preaching and teaching about love, and he doesn't even love his own daughter."

"Jules don't say that. Daddy loves you. I know he does; he's just stubborn, and he thinks in his mind that you are serving the devil, but he loves you, sis," she said picking up a photo of them when they were kids. She rubbed Juliana's face on that picture and wished she could touch her for real.

"Lia, don't make excuses for him, okay? We are twenty-seven-year-old grown women, and you've never even left the state of Georgia. Some things you tell me about Daddy have me shaking my head. He still treats you like a child, Lia, and I cannot comprehend how you and our sisters can take that and not just want to get outta there. We are not seventeen anymore, and Daddy has to realize that we are adults and we have to find our own way."

"He does, Jules, and I know Daddy can be a bit extra, but he loves us, sis, and that is the only way Daddy knows how to be. Yes, he still runs the men away as if we were fifteen, but I don't want to run away. You've been gone for so long, and it's like you refuse to come home to make amends with Daddy, and I'm sure if you just come home and let him see your face, Daddy would wrap his arms around you and things would be fine. Do you know how many times Daddy has called me Jules since you've been gone?"

"Lia, we're twins, identical twins, and Daddy is old. He just gets our names mixed up, like he always has."

"Jules, you know Momma and Daddy know us apart. All I'm saying is come home. You've been gone too long. I wanna see you; our sisters miss you too."

"Ha, what a joke," she said and laughed. The only one that talks to her is Julia and her other sisters were just as self-righteous as her daddy, and if he knew she and Julia still talked as much, he'd hit the ceiling.

"Jules, they love you," Julia said softly.

"No, Lia—you love me. Momma loved me and understood me. That's why she helped me, and she wrote me and talked to me when I was in New York struggling to make it. She tried telling Daddy before she died that he was wrong, but he didn't listen, and now she's gone and you are all I have, Lia. Momma knew how important singing and performing are to me. I just wish she was here to see me now."

"Jules, you talk sometimes like you forget that Momma is in heaven and she can see you now," she said bringing her sister back to what they were taught to believe in.

"Lia, I haven't forgotten. I just sometimes don't believe what Daddy taught us all those years are true."

"Juliana—watch your mouth. You know God is real, and you are not going to go there with me. Now I love you, and you know I support you in whatever you do, but I never want to hear that craziness again. When did you stop believing, Jules? Where's your Bible that Momma gave you? Do you not recall praying to God to bless your music career? I even prayed for that, so don't ever say that again. You are where you are right now because God has allowed it. You know nothing moves, creeps, or exists unless He says so, good or bad, so don't forget where you come from, because God has a way of showing you who He is, and I would hate for Him to show up on your doorstep angry," she said, and Juliana knew she was right, but didn't want to hear it.

"Okay, Lia, okay, please, no sermons, okay?—you sound like Daddy," she said opening her nightstand and retrieving the

Bible she owned for so many years that her momma gave her before she stepped on the bus to go to New York. She used to study and pray back then, but now she couldn't remember the last time she opened it. She sat on her bed and opened it to a family photo of her dad, mom, her, and her four sisters. She rubbed her finger over Julia's face thinking the same thing Julia was thinking, how she missed her so much.

"Okay, I'm not going to preach. I just love you so much, and I'm praying for you day in and day out," Julia said smiling at the picture of them.

"I know, and I love you too, sis, and I miss you so much. You are pretty much the only family I have, so please say you'll come. Daddy ain't gonna like it, but you're a grown woman, and for me can you just let Daddy be angry? By the time you get back, he'll be over it."

"All right, all right, I'll come. It's been almost ten years, and I'm dying to see what you look like in person. Seeing you on TV is so different. I mean, everybody knows here in town that we are twins, but they frown at me, like I'm just a nobody," she said putting the picture back on her nightstand.

"Well, you are not just a nobody, and everyone is going to flip when you come out here and they see I have an identical twin sister," she said putting the picture back into the Bible and putting it back into her nightstand drawer.

"You mean no one knows about me, Juliana?"

"No, no one knows. I never talk about home to anyone. They don't know about any of my relatives and family. They just know me as Juliana and that's that, but that is all about to change. Trust I didn't lie because I was ashamed; I just didn't want to bring shame to Daddy," she said being honest. She had everyone believing she was from New York and she had no siblings and her only family was her momma, who passed away. She went to her momma's funeral, but she was in disguise and no one knew she was there. She wanted to hug her sisters, but she knew her daddy would have been outraged for her to be there, so she sat way in the back with a wig, hat, and large sunglasses.

When Julia told her that their mom died she was messed up for a while. Although she refused over the phone to come to her momma's funeral in fear of her daddy's reaction, as soon as she hung up the phone with Julia she called the airlines and booked a flight. She went to Georgia first, and then to London for a couple months, to grieve to keep her past as private as she could from the world. She was relieved that no one from her Bible belt hometown cared about her career. Since no one knew she lied about not having a family back home, there were never any issues or questions.

"That is like crazy, but I guess you're right. No one has ever approached me with a camera mistaking me for you, but I haven't been anywhere outside of town," she said and thought that was truly sad.

"Well, I can't wait to see you and to show you the world outside of Pastor Valentine," she joked, and they laughed the same laugh. They were a split image standing side by side, and they even sounded the same, and they both sang like angels.

"I'll be there," she said, and they talked another twenty minutes or so, and then Juliana had to go. She showered and got ready to go to dinner with her boyfriend Miles and his son Trey. When she got to the table in the restaurant she was embarrassed that Trey had on his Little League baseball uniform and she wondered why Miles brought him to dinner with that on.

"Miles, this is a joke, right?" she asked with attitude.

"What, baby, what's wrong?" he asked wondering what the problem was.

"This, Trey in his uniform . . . This is an upscale restaurant, and he is sitting here in this," she said holding her hand up in embarrassment.

"Jules, he is a ten-year-old kid, okay, and we didn't have time to go home and be on time for dinner," he said looking at her like she was crazy.

"We won our game today," Trey said.

"Good, congratulations," she said with attitude looking at Miles and not acknowledging Trey with a look or smile.

"Look, Juliana, if you want to go, we can go, but Trey and I are starving, and I told him we would have a victory dessert to celebrate his win."

"Well, I'm not sure if I'll have time for dessert," she said picking up her menu.

"And why not?" he asked wondering why she was always such a bitch, and especially around his son.

"Well, I have a little show tonight, and I have to be there by nine," she said looking at her watch.

"Show—what show? You didn't tell me about a show."

"I know, it was last minute, but Reg called me this afternoon and asked me to swing by this club and do one or two songs, so now I have a show tonight."

"Well, if you have to be there by nine, that means I won't make it, because I won't have time to get Trey home, and then back to your gig," he said a little disappointed. He loved to hear Juliana sing, and he wished he had known a little earlier.

"I tried calling you a couple hours ago, but I only got your voice mail."

"Well, you know when I'm at one of Trey's games, I'm not on the phone," he said telling her for the hundredth time.

"That's the reason why you didn't know," she said not looking up from her menu. "Are you ready to order?" she asked, and he picked up his menu.

"Trey, do you know what you want to have, son?" Miles asked.

Looking up from his handheld game, he replied, "Yea, a cheeseburger and fries," he said and put his head back down.

"Well, Trey . . . This restaurant doesn't make cheeseburgers and fries. That, my dear, is at McDonald's," Juliana said breaking his little heart.

"What do you mean no cheeseburgers and fries? Everybody makes cheeseburgers and fries," he said looking at her with a sad face.

"Well, not here," she said with no remorse like he wasn't ten.

"Look, Trey—they make spaghetti and meatballs. You like spaghetti and meatballs, son," Miles said taking his son's attention from the evil one. "Would you like to have that?"

"Yea, I guess if that's all they have. Why did we come to this place, Dad, if they don't have burgers and fries?"

"Because Juliana loves this place," he said, but Trey didn't care. He didn't like her because she was always so mean, and he didn't understand why his dad liked her, because he sure didn't.

"Well, this place sucks," he said and went back to his game.

"And you suck. Now what?" she spat.

"Come on, Jules, don't—," Miles said because he always had to have that conversation with her about how mean she was to his son and he didn't like it.

"Come on, what? . . . He started it," she said like an immature brat.

"Whatever, Jules. What club are you performing at tonight?" he asked.

"I don't know. Reg is having a car take me over there when we're done for sound check. Far as I know it's a little intimate setting, for some collars, you know," she said and was glad the waiter came over because the only audience that was going to be there for her performance was Reginald. They ordered and ate and ended dinner on a pleasant note.

"So will you be by tonight after your show?" he asked leaning in close to her.

"I'll let you know. It depends on how late I am," she said knowing she wouldn't.

"Okay, then, I'll see you later," he said and kissed her.

"Okay," she smiled, and he closed the door. "Driver, you know our next stop," she told him, and the driver knew to take her to her little condo that she and Reg met up at to do what they do. She made herself a drink and sat back and enjoyed the ride. Soon, she closed her eyes and dreamed of her and Reginald being husband and wife. She was his biggest star, and she knew that they could be the next hottest couple, like Jay-Z and Beyoncé . . . if she could get him to leave Lisa Towers. She was the first lady in Reginald's life and that was the role Juliana wanted to play.

She didn't want a piece of the pie, she wanted the whole pie. She set out the day she signed with that label to get him and nothing was going to stop her. She liked Miles, but Miles was not Reginald Towers. He had millions, but so did Juliana. That's why no matter how sweet and loving Miles was she didn't want the small fish. She seduced Reginald and got him into her web and now her mission was to take him away from Lisa for good.

Chapter Two

"YES, BABY, yes, that's so good," she moaned while Reg's man stroked her insides. She squeezed her thighs tight and enjoyed the loving he was giving her. She wanted their thing to be a permanent thing so she could stop touring all over the world and sit back and enjoy it all like Lisa did. She brought that company millions, and she was already tired and ready to retire. She had an agenda that had her living in the mansion Lisa lived in. She knew it was only a matter of time before she was going to make that happen because Reginald was stone cold and he wasn't an easy win so she was going to have to put on the show of her life if she was going to take him from Lisa Towers.

"You okay?" he asked because Juliana was quieter than usual.

"Yes, I'm okay; well, I hope I'm going to be okay," she said ready to tell him the best news of his life.

"You don't look okay. You look like you just lost your best friend and after what just went down you should be smiling from ear to ear," he said and got up to go to the kitchen to get himself a beer, and when he came back she was ready to tell him.

"Reg, come sit down, baby," she said. He looked around for his boxers and wondered what she wanted this time.

"Juliana, spit it out, baby. I know you're getting ready to ask me for something. What is it, baby? A new car, a trip, shopping spree? What do you want, baby?" he asked and leaned over to kiss her.

"I want you to sit down so we can talk," she said, and he sat down. Juliana was beautiful, and he cared for her, and if things were different, he'd make her his first lady because she was not only beautiful but had a voice of gold, and Reg knew he had to keep her happy to keep her making the company the money that she made. "Do you love me, baby?"

"Of course, I do, you know I do for the hundredth time."

"Then why won't you divorce Lisa and marry me? You know you don't love her like you love me, and I know her stuck-up ass ain't sucking your dick like I suck your dick."

"Jules, please, we've had this discussion a thousand times. I can't leave Lisa, and I don't know why you keep coming at me with this. It's like you can't be happy for shit, Jules. You are the number-one R&B female artist in the world. You live an affluent life. I give you whatever you want, yet you're still not content."

"I want you, Reg, and I want to be on your arm at the awards. I want what we have to be public, and I'm so tired of sneaking around with you and Miles, poor Miles. I hate doing this to him. I hate pretending to love him, and I don't. I love you, Reg, and I want to be your wife. I know you give me everything, but it's not enough. I want you for me, and Lisa is a bitch, and every time she sees me she gives me attitude."

"Lisa is like that with any woman that is around me, Jules, so please, baby, I don't want to hurt you, but I will never leave my wife, and if you can't get that through your head, you and I may need to chill," he said, and she couldn't believe her ears.

"What . . . what, Reggie? You know that's not what I want. You are the only man for me, and you know this. Tell me, do you like me being with Miles?"

"No, but you have to be. Miles is the greatest song writer in history, and if he knew that you and I were together he'd be gone, and I am not ready to give up any of what I have or what we have. Now, come on, baby, let's not talk about this anymore, okay? Let's just enjoy what we have and continue to make each other happy the way we have and just chill, baby," he said kissing her tenderly.

"Reg, I'm afraid things are going to be different," she said because she had to tell him.

"Different how?" he asked wondering what she was up to.

"Because I'm pregnant," she said, and Reginald almost passed out.

"You're what!" he yelled getting up from the bed.

"Pregnant, baby. You're finally going to have a baby. You're finally going to be a daddy," she said hoping he'd be thrilled.

"No, no, how could you get pregnant, Juliana? I trusted you were taking birth control. You know damn well a baby is not what I want."

"Then why is Lisa paying top dollar to see fertility specialists around the damn globe if you don't want a child, Reg?"

"Hey, that is me and my wife's business, Juliana. What we are doing has nothing to do with your ass, and it's not your damn business!" he yelled. He was furious because every time they spoke of children he made it clear that a baby would be a bad idea and it would mess up everything, and she goes and breaks the agreement they had.

"Don't yell at me, Reg," she cried. "I'm sorry, okay? I just thought you'd be happy. I thought this would be good news for you. I thought—," she cried.

"Why would you think something so crazy like that when I've stressed to you how important your career is and it would be bad not only for your career, but people's lives will be destroyed if we brought a baby into this," he said pacing, because he had too much to lose if it got out that she was pregnant by him and that was a bad thing for her to be pregnant.

"I'm sorry, Reg, please, baby, don't be mad. It's going to work out. It's probably better this way. Lisa will leave, and you and I—," she tried to say but he cut her off.

"Juliana, are you out of your fucking mind? It's not that simple, and you are going to ruin my marriage!" he yelled.

"Reggie, this is our child," she cried.

"No, this is your child. How do I know it's mine? You have been with Miles; it could be his. How do you know it's not his?"

"Because Miles uses condoms. Miles sees that I'm not too fond of his son, so he knows that the last thing I want to do is have his child, Reg. Why would you say that? You and I have been together for forever, and you know I've been in love with you since the first time I laid eyes on you. You are the one who told me to get with Miles. That wasn't my idea and to make you happy I did what you asked. I did what was best for business," she cried.

"Yes, you did, but then what did you do, Jules? You go and get pregnant—do you think that was good for business?"

"I thought this would be good for us, Reg. I was thinking of us," she said sobbing.

"No, you were thinking of yourself because you know this is not what I wanted, and I don't need this shit right now. Look, I love you, Juliana, but you can't have this baby."

"Why?"

"Because this will ruin everything!" he shouted, and she was confused. He was on top of the world, and all he had to do was leave Lisa and marry her and raise their baby.

"For who, Reggie? I know you love me, and I know this baby is a good thing," she said trying to touch his face.

"Get rid of it," he said coldly and pushed her hands away.

"What? You can't be serious."

"I am dead serious. You cannot have this baby, and I'll have an appointment set up by the end of this week," he said and started to dress.

"No," she said because there was no way another man was going to make her have another abortion. That would be her third one, and she wasn't going to go through with another abortion.

"Juliana, I'm not fucking around. You are not having this baby."

"Yes, I am, and I'm not having an abortion. I can't believe you'd asked me to do that, Reggie," she cried in disbelief.

"I'm not asking you, I'm telling you."

"No, please, baby, please don't do this to our baby, please," she begged with her face drenched with tears.

"At the end of the week," he said and stepped into his shoes.

"I will not, Reginald, and if you try to make me, I will go to Lisa and tell her."

"Don't fucking threaten me, Juliana. You do not want to fuck with me. Trust me, you do not want to fuck with me," he said walking up on her like he was about to hit her dead in her face, and it scared her.

"Please, I don't want this to get ugly. I want to work this out. You, me, and the baby can be a family. You have nothing to lose; we can be happy," she said reaching for his hands, but he snatched them away.

"Listen, Juliana, you are beautiful, and you are at the height of your music career. Do you know how a baby is going to change everything? You are not ready to be a mom, and you know it. To get pregnant to get me wasn't the answer, so let it go. This baby is not going to be born, you hear me? Now I'll be in touch," he said and walked out.

She yelled out his name, but he kept on going. She hated him for what he had done to her and wanted to hurt him just as bad as he had hurt her. She was devastated that he wanted her to get rid of her baby, and she knew she had to do something to make him understand how much she wanted to be Mrs. Towers. Her child was going to be the start of his legacy, and he wasn't going to make her get rid of her baby no matter what he thought.

She got up and showered and headed back to her house. When she got home she listened to her voice mail. She was happy to hear her sister's voice telling her that she could come by the end of the week. She was happy because she didn't want to be alone, and there was no one else she could tell at that moment about her pregnancy. She called her sister back, and Julia could feel something was wrong.

"Jules, what is it?"

"Nothing, darling, I'm fine."

"You're lying—I can feel it when you're sad, plus I've been having some weird nausea going on, so out with it," Julia demanded.

"Lia, babe, don't worry, because I'm fine. I'm just a little tired. I had a show this evening so I'm just a little worn out, that's all, but your sister is fine," she said lying.

"No, Jules, there is something else. I can feel it."

"Listen, I'll call you tomorrow about your flight information and we'll talk when you get here, okay?"

"You sure? Because I'll be happy to listen now," she offered.

"No, sis, get some sleep and I'll call you tomorrow."

"Okay, Jules, I love you, and I can't wait to see you," Julia said.

"You too, sis, I can't wait 'til you get here," she said, and they hung up. The next day she got up and made arrangements for her sister to come out to L.A.

Chapter Three

JULIANA WAS counting down the days for Julia's arrival. She was so excited she couldn't contain herself. She ignored Reg's phone calls, and he wasn't happy that she was going against the grain. Juliana knew she was going to go public with her pregnancy, but she didn't want to do anything to ruin her sister's visit. She made sure her schedule was clear for the entire two weeks that her sister was going to be there. She wanted to show her sister the time of her life, and she wasn't going to have anything negative interfering with Julia's visit.

"Jules!" Reg yelled from the foyer when he walked into Juliana's house.

"Yes?" Juliana responded coming out of the kitchen and wondered why he didn't call before he came.

"Hey, babe," Reggie said.

"What do you want, Reggie?"

"I wanted to talk to you."

"About what, Reg? You said all you had to say the other night," she stated not wanting to see him.

"Come on, Jules, you know you're my favorite girl. I've been calling, and you've been ignoring my calls, and I want us to settle this," he said moving close to her, but she was not in the mood.

"Reg, what do you want?" she asked giving him attitude.

"No 'hey, baby, what's up?' No kiss?" he said laying on the charm.

"Hey, baby, what's up?" she said and gave him a peck. "Now what do you want?"

"Well, I came by to check on you and to see when you were planning to take care of this situation."

"What situation?" she snapped.

"Come on, Jules, you know this has to be done as quickly as possible. This is something we should not wait to have done."

"Well, I don't have a situation. I'm pregnant, Reg. That is not a situation. We are having a baby," she said walking past him. She knew she was pregnant, but she grabbed a glass and poured some wine.

"So that's it? I don't get a say in this?"

"Yea, you do, Reg, and you've said enough. I'm not having the abortion, so if that is not the answer you wanna hear this conversation is over," she said and took a sip of the wine, and his jaw tightened. He rubbed his head and tried to calm himself because he wanted to choke her.

"Juliana—why in the fuck are you doing this? You have everything, and any woman in the world would die to be who you are, and instead of you going with the program and doing the responsible thing, you want to cause havoc for everyone. Now can you stop being so fucking difficult and have the damn abortion? You knew from the jump that I had a wife, and you know getting pregnant is the first rule not to break when you are fucking a married man, and you broke that rule, and I'll be damn if I let you fuck things up for me by having a baby!" he yelled scaring her.

"Fine, Reggie, now get the fuck out!" she yelled.

"So you gon' do it?" he asking, pleading.

"Get out!" she yelled.

"Jules, please, you can't keep this baby," he cried hoping he'd get through to her.

"Get out!" she yelled again moving toward him.

"Look, Juliana, you can't, okay? You just can't!" he yelled, but she didn't care.

"Reg, I'm keeping my baby, and you can't make me terminate this pregnancy. Like it or not you are going to be a dad, and however you want this to turn out is on you, now please just go."

"Jules . . .," he said disappointed in her.

"I'm not going to change my mind, Reggie," she said, and he didn't say anything else. He knew she was a force to be reckoned with, and he knew he was going to have to handle her in a different way.

■ ■

"Hey, sis—oh my God, I can't believe how beautiful you are," Julia said hugging her sister. She looked amazing, and although they were identical, Julia knew that there was definitely a difference between them from the clothes to the hair to the overall package.

"You are just as beautiful. Look at you. I can't believe my eyes. It's like looking at myself without my makeup. We have to get you to the spa right now," Juliana told Julia, ready to get her out of those frumpy clothes and glasses. She looked just like Juliana, except there was no glam.

"Man, do I look that bad?" Julia asked grabbing her dress that was down to her ankles, looking like a church girl.

"No, sweetie, you are beautiful. You look just like me," she teased, and they laughed. "Come on, let's get your luggage so we can get you out of these grandma clothes."

"Okay," she said excited. Juliana looked like a star, and there was no way Julia could look as good as she, she thought to herself as they rode to Juliana's manor. When they pulled up to the gate Julia thought she was in a dream. "Jules, this is not your house," she said in disbelief.

"Oh, yes, it is," she said, and Julia thought she was going to pee on herself.

"Get out of town! This house is bigger than my block."

"Wait 'til you see the inside," her sister said and pulled into the garage.

"Oh my God, Jules, this is gorgeous, and oh my God, it's huge. Why do you have a house this size just for you? Jessica, Jada, and Janice would die if they saw this house. You have five bathrooms, and oh my God, you have a vanity. I have always wanted to sit at a vanity and put on my makeup," she said as they walked through the entire house admiring everything. Julia sat at her sister's vanity in excitement touching everything.

"You actually wear makeup?" Juliana asked teasing.

"Yes, on Sundays," she said, and they cracked up.

"Come on, let me show you to your room," Juliana said, and Julia followed her into another master with a bathroom and vanity, and she knew two weeks wasn't going to be enough time for her to enjoy the luxurious things in her sister's home.

"Jules, you have a pool and hot tub," she said opening the French doors that led out to a balcony overlooking the back of the house.

"Yes, ma'am. Even though I have it, I never get in it," she said pulling the curtains open so her sister could see the beautiful view.

"Why not?"

"Chile, please, I ain't messing up my hair with that waadah," she said sounding like the country girl Julia remembered.

"Oh, Jules, it's so good to see you, sis," she said, and they hugged again.

"You too, Lia. I'm so glad you are here, now come on, let's get your bags so we can get you changed and go out and see L.A.," Juliana said, and they went and got her bags. After going through Julia's entire suitcase, Juliana grabbed her arm and took her into her walk-in closet. She found something suitable for her to wear, and they sang together as Julia changed. They were both smiling from ear to ear as Julia came out of the bathroom, still holding a note from one of Juliana's songs, and Juliana was impressed that she held the note longer than she did, but she didn't say anything; she just smiled, because she knew Julia's voice was always a bit stronger than hers.

She gave Julia two thumbs-up to the cute sundress she put on that showed some skin, and they were off. Juliana wanted to try to keep a low profile and wasn't ready to show her sister off, so she called the spa ahead and said she needed some beauty treatments to get back to normal. She lied and said she had been out of the country for a few weeks and she was a mess.

She pulled up front and sent Julia in without her and immediately when she walked in they took her for Juliana and Julia didn't say a word; she just enjoyed the special treatments. While she was getting prettied up Juliana was at the nearby shops grabbing her sister some new clothes to wear and told herself that all the clothes that Julia brought with her would be picked up by the Salvation Army.

When Juliana came back to get Julia she was please with her makeover and it was like looking at herself in the mirror and her jaw dropped at how gorgeous her sister was. Even though her sister now looked presentable to be in L.A., Juliana still wasn't ready to introduce her just yet so she ordered her favorite dish from her favorite restaurant and picked it up to go. They drove around the city a bit, and then headed back to the house where Juliana introduced her sister to apple martinis.

"Jules, no, you know I don't drink the devil's nectar," Julia said.

"What did I tell you before you came? There is no sin in Cali, so come on, live a little. I promise I won't tell Daddy," she said, and they laughed like they were kids.

"Jules, I've never had a drink in my life," she said afraid to even try it.

"Lia, it is only an apple martini. I promise it won't hurt you, lil sis; come on, try it," Juliana said and Julia gave in. After a couple drinks and some good eating they were giggling and reminiscing about their childhood growing up in the Valentine house. Julia was drunk off three drinks, but she was happy and having a good time. They sang, danced, and had a great time catching up.

"Oh my God, Jules, if Daddy could see me now, with the hair and makeup and this sexy momma dress, he'd go crazy," she said laughing and fell back onto her sister's bed.

"I know, and he'd be blaming me too, just like he used to when we were little. 'Jules, it's because of you that Lia did this,' or 'Jules, you know everything you do your sister does and you're a bad example,'" she said mocking her father.

"You know, part of what Daddy said was true."

"Was it?" she asked.

"Yes, everything you are doing I've wanted to do, but never had the courage to do it."

"Well, you can always come out here and start over, Lia. I am more than okay, and you wouldn't have to worry about anything. I'd take care of you until you accomplished whatever you want to," she said sitting on the bed and taking Julia by the hand. She really wished she'd stay so she could have some family with her.

"Naw, I can't stay. This is your life not mine. I belong in Georgia at my school, teaching music to my students," she said putting her head down. She loved her life, but wouldn't mind trading it in to live like her sister lived.

"You belong wherever you want to be, so just remember at any time, just say the word and it's done. I know you love teaching, but you can teach here. You can sing here. There are churches here, Lia, and you can do whatever you wanna do. I am more than okay," she said, and they hugged.

"I know I'm welcome. I just hope I'm welcome back home when these two weeks are over," she sighed.

"What? What happened? Did Daddy give you a hard time?"

"Your Daddy told me not to ever come home if I got on the plane to come see you," she said, and her eyes watered.

"Awww, sis, why didn't you tell me before?" she asked with her eyes welling too. She knew how her daddy was, but she didn't want her dad to disown Julia, like he disowned her.

"Because, Jules, you're right. We are adults now, and no one wants to defy him, but he can't stop me from living, and no matter what he said to me last night, nothing was going to stop me from getting on that plane today to come here to see you," she said, and Juliana hugged her really tight.

"I love you, sis, and this is like the best day of my life, seeing you again. I've missed you more than I ever missed anyone on this planet, and remember, it's your choice. If you want to stay, stay. If you decide to go back, I won't stop you. Just know I have your back. You are my other half, and I feel whole again for a change. The offer will always be on the table."

"Thank you, Jules. This is by far the happiest day of my life, and while I'm here, I will think about what I want, and if I choose to stay or go . . . you will be the first to know. Now help me to my room, because between these sexy momma shoes and those three drinks I may fall," she said, and Juliana helped her to her room. She helped her drunken sister into her nightgown and into bed. She kissed her and told her again how happy she was to have her there and went to bed.

Chapter Four

JULIANA SAT up in the bed because she heard a noise. She lay back down because she figured it was Julia going to the kitchen for something. Then she heard another noise, and she thought she should get up and make sure Julia was okay. She opened Julia's door and saw her still in the bed, and she wondered what that noise was. She stood still, and her heart began to race. She hoped no one was in her house and didn't want to wake her sister because she didn't want to scare her, her first night in California.

She also wondered if it was Reg because besides Elsa, her housekeeper, he was the only one who knew her gate and alarm code. She moved down the stairs, slowly tiptoeing so she wouldn't wake her sister, and when she reached the bottom, Reg turned on the light.

"Oh my God, Reg, you scared the shit out of me. What are you doing here at this hour? I told you we had nothing more to discuss," she said putting her hands on her hips, keeping her voice down.

"I know what you said, Jules, and like I told you, you can't have this baby," he said moving toward her. "Who else knows about this pregnancy? Did you go to the doctor?"

"No one knows, Reg. I did a home test, and I plan to see a doctor soon," she said and moved away. She didn't want him to touch her.

"Listen . . . I tried to reason with you, but you don't wanna hear me. I have a doctor that will keep this thing here—our little secret. All I need you to do is go upstairs, get dressed, and we can have this done by morning. Now this is costing me a hefty penny, Jules, and I didn't come here to take no for an answer," he said, and she laughed in his face.

"Reg, you can't make me do anything, so get the hell out of my house," she said, keeping her voice down again, and he wondered why she was whispering.

"Are you with someone? Do you have a niggah upstairs or something? I didn't see a vehicle of Miles's out front."

"I don't have a man in my bed, okay, Reg, now please just go," she said moving to the door and when she opened it, there were unexpected faces greeting her. "Who the hell are you?" she blurted, and Reg spoke up.

"Jules, we cannot have this baby, now either you come with me willingly or . . ." he warned, and she folded her arms defiantly.

"I'm not going anywhere with you, understand? Now get the hell out!" she yelled hoping she wouldn't wake her sister.

"Well, you leave me no choice," he said, and when they tried to grab her she fought and broke loose. Before she could make it to the staircase, one of the guys grabbed her. She tried to fight him off, but he was too strong. She bit his arm, and he threw her to the floor. She screamed and tried to crawl away, but another man grabbed her ankles and dragged her back.

"Please, please, I'm pregnant, please," she begged and was able to scramble back to the steps. She ran up, trying to get to her gun in her nightstand, but they were on her and threw her to the floor again. Even though she told them she was pregnant that didn't stop one of the men from trying to restrain her and poke a needle in her arm, but she fought and she screamed and that caused him to drop the needle.

Julia heard her yell, and she jumped up and ran to see what was going on. The men were distracted because they had no idea she was there, and that allowed Juliana time to rise to her feet, but Rocky, one of Reg's men, pushed her, and she fell back and hit her head on her marble nightstand. She fell to the floor hard, unconscious.

"Reg," Rocky yelled, and then Buster grabbed Julia, because she tried to run away. Reg rushed up to the second floor and when he saw the scene, he was confused as hell.

"What are you doing, and who the hell is this?" Reg asked when he saw Juliana lying on the floor unconscious and Buster holding someone that looked exactly like her. Buster removed his hand so she could answer.

"What did you do to her? Who are you?" she cried looking at her sister's motionless body on the floor.

"Take her to the car now!" Reg ordered in a panic.

"Rocky, get Jules," he said, and Rocky hurried to do what he was told. Julia tried to keep the man from restraining her and dragging her to the car, but she couldn't. She kicked and screamed, and he put his hand over her mouth. He dragged her down the steps although she struggled to get away. Rocky picked up Juliana's limp body from the floor, and he followed Reggie down the steps, not realizing Juliana's head was dripping blood. They took them to the car, and Buster forced Julia to get in.

Julia was shaking like a leaf. He put Juliana in, and when her head landed in Julia's lap, she screamed at the sight of her sister's blood. When Rocky realized she was bleeding, he instructed Buster to go back in for a wet towel and told Julia to hold it against the back of Juliana's head. She cried for her sister to wake up, but she wouldn't open her eyes. She checked and saw that she was still breathing, but the blood still leaked from the back of her head, and Julia was terrified.

Reg looked around the place and was confused. Julia had taken him by surprise. He did not expect anyone to be there, and she was a split image of Juliana. He thought his eyes had to be playing tricks, but that was another matter, because he noticed the blood trail.

"Take them out to the cabin right now, and I'll meet you guys there. Doctor Pollkalski will be there to look at Juliana. Now go," he ordered, and he knew he had to clean up his mess and get to the bottom of what was going on.

"What did she do? Why did you hurt my sister?" Julia cried, holding Juliana tight after they pulled out of the drive.

"Bitch, shut your fucking mouth!" Rocky yelled.

"Rocky, chill, dude, damn," Buster said because he was nervous as hell. Things had gone way wrong, and he was just as terrified as Julia. The ride felt like an eternity for Julia, and all she did was pray and beg God to let her sister be okay. She cried and held her sister the entire ride, begging her to wake up, and by the time they got to their destination, the towel was drenched with blood and Juliana's pulse was faint.

"Please, sir, my sister is dying. We need to go to a hospital," Julia said when he turned off the ignition in front of a huge house in the back of a wooded area. By then, Julia was shaking uncontrollably. She thought this was the end of her life too, since she had a feeling that her sister had bled to dead.

Rocky instructed Buster to carry Juliana's body in. Two hours later, Reg finally showed up and didn't believe his eyes when he saw Julia. She was sitting there trembling with blood all over her gown, and Reggie wanted to know what they did with Juliana. He told Julia to sit tight, and then followed Rocky into another room where Julia imagined her sister was dying. Reg came back into the front and told Buster to take Julia upstairs.

"No, no, please, no," Julia screamed and tried to fight, but it was no use. He took her upstairs and threw her onto the bed in one of the rooms. "Please, don't, please, sir. I promise if you just let me and my sister go I will not say a word. God is my witness. I won't. I want to make sure my sister is okay," she said talking to Buster, but he didn't reply or say a word. He just left her in the room and shut the door.

She got up and ran to the window. Even if she could get it open, how was she going to get down from the second floor? She searched the room for a phone, but there was no phone. She grabbed the doorknob, but paused because she was not strong enough to take down three men.

After about thirty minutes Rocky came back with an oversized shirt and told her to take off the bloody gown and put on the tee shirt. At first she refused, but he pulled out a handgun, and she immediately stood and changed right in front of him. She handed him the soiled gown, and he left her in the room again. She fell on her knees and began to pray. She didn't know what else to do. She prayed for hours, and finally, she fell over and went to sleep. A few hours later, she woke up and had to pee really badly. She went over to the door, opened it, and yelled for someone to come. After about two minutes, Rocky finally came.

"I have to use the bathroom really bad," she said and he waved for her to follow him. He took her to the bathroom and stood outside until she was done. She could barely hold on to her liquid as she squatted over the toilet to relieve her bladder. She looked at herself and noticed her sister's dried up blood was stained on her body, so she washed her hands for what seemed like an eternity.

When she opened the door, Rocky was standing there. "Where is my sister? Is she okay?" she asked, but he just walked away expecting her to follow him, but she wouldn't move. "I'm not going back into that room until you tell me where my sister is," she cried, and he just grabbed her and pushed her back in the room and shut the door. She began to cry and pace and pray. After what seem like forever the door opened. It was Reg.

"Who are you?" she asked.

"Well, little lady, please let me ask the questions and you answer me," he ordered. She sat on the bed. "What is your name?"

"Julia," she said with watery eyes.

"Julia, don't cry, okay? I'm not going to hurt you, I promise, so relax," he said, but she was still shaking. "Come on, relax. I'm not going to hurt you. Not if you cooperate with me. You'll be just fine."

"What do you want from me, and why did you hurt my sister?" she cried, scared to death.

"Hey, I said I'll ask the questions, okay?" he said, and she looked away and her tears fell. "Now, looking at you, looking exactly like Juliana, I take it you are her twin sister," he said. Julia didn't respond. "Listen, Julia, this can be easy or hard. No one in L.A. knows anything about Juliana having a twin sister, and you, baby, are more than just a twin. You look like a photocopy of her. I mean, your resemblance is unbelievable. I've seen twins in my day, but never ever have I seen such a remarkable resemblance. If you two were standing side by side,

I would only know Jules because you got her by five or ten pounds," he said still in total disbelief.

"Okay, and what?" she said crying. "Where is my sister? Please tell me if she's all right."

"Hold on, remember, I ask the questions," he said handing her a tissue to wipe her face. "Where are you from, Julia?"

"Georgia," she said with her head down.

"How long have you been here in California?"

"Since yesterday."

"How long is your trip?"

"Two weeks," she said crying.

"Well, here is the thing, Ms. Julia. My boys put me in a really bad situation. I didn't plan for the night to go the way it did, and I'm going to need you to do something for me," he said, and she thought maybe he was out of his mind to be asking her for favors when he couldn't tell her if her sister was dead or alive.

"Something like what?" she asked, wondering what she could possibly do for him.

"I'm going to need you to be Juliana," he said, and she began to blink profusely, because she couldn't believe her ears.

"Be Juliana . . . come again. Why? What did you do to her? What did you do to her?" she yelled, jumping up trying to run to the door, but he was on her like white on rice and grabbed her. "Jules, Jules!" she yelled reaching for the door, but he dragged her back and threw her down on the bed sobbing.

"Listen, Julia, I just told you, you can make this hard or easy," he said, and she sobbed uncontrollably. "Look, be quiet and listen to me," he demanded. "I didn't want it to come to this, but that bitch left me with no choice. Now you have two choices. Either you do what I'm telling you, or you're going to end up like Juliana," he said, and she was more afraid than she ever was in her life.

"And . . . if . . . I . . . say . . . no?" she said between sobs. He stood up.

"Well, I'm going to go downstairs and let you think about it for a while," he said and left her there shaken and scared to death. He was gone for hours, and she was starving and had to go to the bathroom again. She banged on the door and yelled for someone, and as soon as Rocky opened the door, she was doing the pee-pee dance.

"Please, I have to go to the bathroom," she said shaking. He stepped to the side to let her by. She was so thirsty when she was done washing her hands she drank the lukewarm water from the faucet. She looked at her face and could not tell that she had gone to the spa the day before. Her reflection reminded her of her sister, and she knew if she was going to get out of there alive she'd have to go along with whatever they said. She grabbed a paper towel from the holder that was on the wall and wiped her face. Then she took a deep breath and opened the door. When she went back into the room, Reg was sitting in the chair waiting for her.

"Are you hungry?"

"Yes," she whispered. She wanted to be stubborn and not ask him for anything, but she had to eat. Beside the fact of her being hungry as hell she needed energy.

"Okay," he said and took his phone out of his pocket. He called downstairs, and Buster brought up a tray of food. She was so happy to see the food she said her grace quickly and ate it before they took it back. Reg sat there patiently until she was done, and then called Buster back up to get the tray. A few moments after she heard a drill on the other side of the door and wondered what they were doing now. She then heard a sound that sounded like a latch locking and then unlocking and she had a bad feeling that they were not letting her leave anytime soon. "So are you ready to talk about my request?"

"Honestly, do I have a choice?" she asked since she couldn't just get up and walk out the door. He laughed.

"Well, actually you do, Julia Samara Valentine. I went back to your sister's place and got your purse, and I found out some things about you and your family. And I know you are not familiar with who I am, but I know a couple of bad guys that wouldn't mind torching your father's church, and you got some pretty sisters that I'm sure you want to remain safe and unharmed," he said threatening her again. All it took was a few phone calls and he had enough information to use as leverage to get Julia to do what he wanted her to do.

"Please don't," she begged.

"That's all on you," he said confident that he had her.

"Look—how do you want me to pass as Juliana? No one is going to believe that I'm her. We even sound different," she said, and he disagreed.

"Well, you sound like her to me, and I knew Juliana well," he said implying she was dead, and Julia covered her mouth. She began to cry again. Reg reclined back in the chair and wondered why she was so torn up about a woman that never mentioned her or her family. Who lied and told everyone she was from New York and she was an only child. He let her cry for a while because he knew she was upset and he was too, but he had to cover his own ass. He didn't want things to blow up in his face, and no matter what he had to do, no one was going to know about Juliana, and he was going to turn Julia into her to keep Towers Records and out of jail for murder. Even though he didn't physically do it, he was responsible for the entire incident, and he'd lose everything behind it, and the fact she was pregnant with his child would only make matters worse.

All he wanted was to convince her to have the procedure done. He had a doctor on hand that he paid well to give Juliana the abortion. He just wanted to get Juliana alone to convince her that that was the best thing to do and if she still didn't agree he'd have to take a more drastic measure by dragging her out of her house and sedating her, so his doctor friend could do the procedure anyway. It was a sick idea, but he knew Juliana wasn't going to give up her baby, so he decided he'd take matters into his own evil hands.

The injection that they were instructed to give her was only a sedative to keep her unconscious for the drive to his vacation home, but things went very wrong. He now would face some serious charges, and that wasn't the plan.

"Listen, your speaking voice sounds the same to me. My question is, can you sing?" he asked, and she nodded. "How well?" he asked. She sang a verse of one of her sister's songs softly, and he smiled. "This is unbelievable. I mean, if I didn't know the truth, I would not know the difference. To look so much like her is insane. I mean, this is going to work," he said amused at his own sick idea. All he had to do was convert Julia into the bitch Juliana was and the singing is a small thing because the studio would take care of that. He just had to teach her how to walk and talk and act like Juliana. He had to turn her into a diva, and he knew he needed time. "So what do you say? Help me and stay alive. Keep your mouth shut and your family will live. Help me and nothing happens to your daddy or his church and we all come out on top."

"My family is expecting me home in two weeks," she said, and he smirked.

"Well, you'll just have to call home and tell your family you've decided to stay a little longer," he said and left her in the room alone again. She heard that sound once more and ran over to the door and tried to open it, but she was locked in. Her heart began to race. She had no idea what she was going to do or how she was going to get out of there and away from Reg. She fell on her knees by the bed and began to pray.

"Father God in heaven, please protect me from my enemies. I'm not afraid, Lord, because I know you are with me, and I know my life is valuable, and I have to do what I have to do until I can get out of this situation, but in the meantime, Lord, give me strength and courage to fight and do whatever it is to allow me and my family to be safe, Lord. Please, Father, in Jesus' name I pray," she said and climbed into the bed. She lay there, and the tears streamed down. Eventually she closed her eyes and fell asleep.

Chapter Five

THE NEXT morning the sound of the door unlocking woke her up. It was Buster letting her out to go to the bathroom.

"Excuse me, sir, Buster, right?" she said remembering what Reg and Rocky called him. "I was wondering if it would be possible to get a toothbrush and maybe something I can shower with. I mean, it's been a couple days, and I really need to shower," she said. He didn't speak, he just nodded. She went to the bathroom, and then he locked her back in the room. She was starving, and the dried up bloodstains on her skin color was even darker than the day before. She wondered if this was Reg's way of showing her who was boss.

After an hour of waiting for someone to come back she heard the door again. This time it was the other guy, Rocky, with a bag. He put the bag on the dresser and stood there with no words. She got up and looked in the bag. In it was some clean clothes and new underwear. It had a toothbrush and toothpaste and all the essentials she needed. She grabbed the bag and went to the bathroom, where there were fresh towels on the vanity.

She showered and watched the bloodstained water go down the drain and wondered what they had done with her sister's body. She wondered if she died or if they ever got her medical attention. She tried not to cry, but she wept again in the shower uncontrollably. She had never been so scared in her entire life. She decided she'd do whatever Reg wanted her to, to save herself and her family. She found the strength to turn off the waterworks and lathered one more time, and then got out, wondering what that day would bring. Julia had no idea where she was or when she was going to be able to go downstairs.

She wondered what happened between Reg and Juliana to make him want her dead. Why would he want to kill her sister? She wondered why Juliana didn't tell her what was going on, and she couldn't figure out why on earth this had to happen to her. All she wanted to get at that point was some answers.

She dressed and was surprised that the man was gone when she came out of the bathroom. She put the bag on the floor by the dresser and sat down in the chair, wondering if they were going to give her a pair of shoes, but then she figured they'd want to keep her from running away. Little did they know she didn't have a problem walking the road barefoot, because that's the way she did it all of her life, and to run through the woods barefoot wouldn't bother her at all to save her life.

She sat there and waited and waited, but no one came up to lock her in. She got up and went into the hall and wondered what the other four rooms on that floor looked like inside and if she was the only prisoner there. She moved slowly to the top of the steps and looked down. Her heart was pounding, but she took the first step down. She paused and asked God for strength and took another step. "Oh Jesus," she said shaking like a leaf and took another, and then another. When she finally made it to the bottom they were sitting in the living room, and she stood there frozen.

"Juliana," Reg said getting up. Julia was frozen. She didn't say anything, she just stood there not knowing what to do or say. Buster and Rocky were sitting at a table smoking and playing cards like they were not holding her hostage upstairs. "Come and sit and join us," he said leading her over to the chair, and she sat. "Are you hungry?" he asked, and she nodded. Buster put down his cards and went into the kitchen and retrieved the Styrofoam container with her meal in it. It was a little cold, but she knew not to complain. Reg sat patiently and let her finish eating, and when she was done, Buster took away her unfinished food.

"Well, we gotta a lot of work to do, but first things first," he said and went to get a cell phone and a pad with something written on it.

"What's this?" she asked.

"Well, this, my little country girl, is a cell phone, and this is what I want you to say," he said handing the pad and phone to her. "Read over this to make sure you got it," he said, and she took the pad and read it. "Now you are going to call Miles and tell him that you had to go away for a while for a family emergency and let him know that you'll be in touch," he instructed her and pulled a gun out. She dropped the phone and moved back.

"Why do you have that? You don't need that," she told him, but he didn't put it away.

"Get the phone, Julia, and call him. This is just to ensure you don't try anything crazy," he stated coldly, and she didn't argue with his crazy ass. She dialed the number from the pad, and Miles picked up on the second ring.

"Hey, Jules, baby, where are you? I've been calling you for the last two days, girl," he said and the tears formed in Julia's eyes. This was a stranger, but he was the first person she spoke to that seemed to care about Juliana.

"Um, Miles, um, hi," she said and cleared her throat and wiped her tears. She looked at the pad and read what it said. "I'm so sorry, baby, but I had to leave town for a family emergency, and um . . .," she said and paused. "I'll be away for a little while," she said trying to sound like she wasn't crying.

"What, what happened, baby? I mean, what family?—I thought you didn't have any family," he said, and she didn't know what to say, because the answer to that wasn't on the paper.

"Um, well, I have an aunt on my mom's side here in New York, and a cousin contacted me the other day, and since she was my momma's only sister I had to fly out here," she said straightening up.

"Wow, I had no idea. Is everything okay? Do you need me to fly out there with you? You know I'd be there in a minute," he offered. Meanwhile, Reg was signaling her to wrap it up.

"No, Miles, I'm fine, so please don't worry about me. I'm fine, okay? I'll be in touch, okay?" she said and ended the call. Reg clapped his hands.

"Oh my God, girl, you are a natural. I see talent runs in the family," he said, and Julia didn't find anything amusing. "Now, here is what we're going to do. You are going to have to learn each and every one of Juliana's songs, and I know you are going to have to get on the treadmill, because you got a nice body, but Juliana was just a tad bit smaller than you, but it won't take you long to get there. Next, I have these DVDs for you to watch. You're going to have to learn how she walks and how she talks, and your sister was a bitch, so this sweet Southern girl image you got going on is going to have to disappear."

"Well, Reg, I have followed my sister's entire career, and I know the words to all of her songs, and I grew up with Juliana. There is not much I don't know about her," Julia said letting him know regardless of what Jules told him, she and Juliana were close and sometimes talked to each other five times a day. She had overheard the way she's talked to people, even when she was being a bitch, so she didn't have a lot to learn about her sister because she knew everything about her except for why Reg wanted her dead.

"Well, good. This shouldn't take too long then," he said and stood.

"Why, Reg, why did you have to kill my sister? She loved you, Reg, and talked about you all the time. She told me how you and she were going to be married one day and how she wanted to have your children, and you killed her. I just need to know what my sister did so evil to you to make you want to take her life," she said with tears streaming, and Reg's eyes watered as well. He did love Juliana, and he never intended for her to be killed, but things went south, and now he had to cover it up.

"Listen, Julia, you need to stop asking me questions, okay? You don't know shit about what Juliana and I had . . . you don't," he expressed, but his two henchmen were sitting there waiting to see their boss crack. "Listen, you just concentrate on doing what it is you need to do if you want to live, all right?" he said and walked out the door. He came back in and took the cell phone out of Julia's hand just in case she got any smart ideas.

Chapter Six

AFTER TEN weeks of video footage, pictures, profiles, rundowns, music videos, and taped interviews and descriptions of all the people Juliana associated with, Julia was now Juliana. She knew everything about everybody, and she just hoped she didn't forget anyone's name. Reg advised her to address those she didn't remember as sweetie or hun, because Juliana was good for calling people that.

She was in the car finally riding back into the city with the two bodyguards and Reg. Reggie was on the phone talking, and Julia was looking out the window at this foreign place. She had only been in Cali for one day before she was kidnapped, and she was wondering how she was going to actually pull it off without someone figuring her out.

Before they went to her sister's house, they went by her stylist's place so he could get her back to beautiful as Reg would say, and Reg told her to pretend she had laryngitis to keep from talking much. Her stylist talked a mile a minute, scolding her for not taking better care of her skin and hair while she was away. He got her back to gorgeous, and when they parted with a big kiss and hug, Julia knew that she was stuck. If her personal stylist, Rob, the man who did her hair and makeup on a regular, couldn't tell she was an imposter, she knew her role as Juliana wasn't going to end soon.

They then went by the studio so Reg could show her around. Although he recorded the entire building and all the personnel, he still wanted to take her by to see if anyone noticed the difference. She walked in just like Juliana would have and gave people a look over her shades the same way Juliana did.

She was so nervous and knew she'd mess up, but once they got into the car to head to her sister's house she was more relaxed. When they pulled in front of the gate, he keyed in the code and made sure Julia had it. When they got inside, he laid down the rules and made sure that he told her the house had surveillance cameras installed and wired for sound, so if she tried anything he'd know.

He told her that she had to keep a tracking device on her at all times and if at any point he could not contact her, he'd make one call and something would happen to her daddy or one of her sisters, and she was terrified. She believed him to be a dangerous man. Although he bluffed her, she had no idea that he wasn't serious. Her sister was already dead, and she didn't know what he did with her body. She still cried, but she knew it was out of her hands. She was just glad to be out of the house out in the country and to have access to other people.

"Now I'm going to leave you to get acquainted with your new home, but keep in mind that I'm watching you," he said pointing out the new cameras. "You are not to drive or go anywhere without Buster," he said placing his hand on one of his goon's shoulders. "If you need anything, Rocky here will get it for you. I will have a couple new round-the-clock bodyguards for you that will not be in on this thing like we are so be sure to keep your damn mouth shut," he said grabbing her face and squeezed tightly. "Understood?" he yelled menacingly.

"Yes," she said and he let her face go with a little push. He grabbed his hat, and Buster and Rocky followed him outside. Julia let out a deep breath. She walked around her sister's massive home and cried. Soon, she sat on the floor and asked God again why was she going through this. At that moment, Buster came in.

"Um, Juliana, I'm going to be in the guesthouse and the extension is 7733. If you have to go anywhere at any time the boss said for you to call me," he told her and walked away.

"Hey, Buster," she called out. He stopped. That was the most he had said to her in ten weeks.

"Yes, Ms. Valentine?" he answered.

"Where is she? Please tell me where she is. Is she okay? I won't tell, I promise, I just need to know she's okay," she begged, but he didn't respond. He just turned and walked away. Julia screamed. She went into her purse and tried to dial a number, but it was blocked. She scrolled through the call list. The phone was programmed for the numbers on the list only, so she threw it on the couch. She went to the house phone, but every time she hit a number, it gave her a fast busy. She dialed the guesthouse extension. It rang, and she figured Reg got her good. He had her phone fixed and cameras throughout the house so she didn't know how she was going to get away. She knew then the lengths a person would go through to cover a murder, and she knew this was only the beginning of her nightmare.

She went upstairs. The house was clean, and the beds were made, and not a drop of blood was evident, so she figured Reg had taken care of that too. She sat on the bed and looked at her sister's closet. She got up and looked at all the clothes and shoes she owned and thought, Damn, Jules was a fashion diva, because she had clothes upon clothes. She opened her lingerie drawers and saw thongs, bras, and camisoles in every color and style. After going through all of her sister's things for about an hour she heard the cell phone downstairs ringing so she ran to answer it.

When she got to it she missed a call from Miles so she called him back. Maybe he could help her, but when he answered, she remembered Reg was listening.

"Hey, baby, you're back?"

"Yea, how'd you know?" she asked.

"Well, I ran into Reg at the studio, and he said they had just dropped you home. Why didn't you call me to pick you up? You know I'm dying to see you."

"Well, when I called to let Reg know I was coming home today he surprised me at the airport. He said you'd be at the studio, but when we went by the studio you weren't there," she said sitting on the sofa.

"Oh, okay. Well, I'm on my way over so I can see you," he said, and she hopped up. She wasn't ready to meet him face to face. She wasn't ready to see him that day, but since he was supposed to be Juliana's boyfriend, she knew he wouldn't take no for an answer.

"Oh, okay, um, I'll be here," she said not knowing what else to say.

"Okay, and, Jules, I have Trey with me," he said.

"Who?" she asked because she forgot that quickly about his son.

"Aw, damn, Jules," he said not believing she said that.

"Miles, baby, I'm joking, okay? I was just kidding," she said with a smile in her voice. She remembered Trey's picture, and she wanted to meet him because she loved kids.

"Oh, okay. We'll be there in about thirty minutes," he said, and they got off the phone. She went upstairs to change. She looked through her sister's wardrobe. There were too many clothes to process, so she grabbed a pair of jeans and a tee shirt. She practiced in the mirror until she heard the intercom buzzing. Quickly, she went over to it and pressed the button.

"Yes?" she said. It was them. She ran down the steps and prayed to God she wouldn't give herself away. She went to the door and opened it after she heard the bell. "Hey," she said, and he walked in and hugged her. He kissed her and put his tongue in her mouth. She didn't expect that, so she backed off quickly.

"Damn, baby, you are looking good. New York has been good to you. Feels like you filled out a little," he said holding on to her tightly.

"Yes, I put on a couple pounds," she said turning her attention to Trey, and that was odd. "Hey, Trey, how are you, dude? It's nice to see you," she said kneeling down to hug him, but he didn't hug her back.

"Wow, New York has truly been good to you," Miles said, and she tilted her head.

"What?" she asked confused.

"Well, you and Trey have not actually been the best of friends."

"No way. This little guy is the coolest," she said, and Trey raised his brow. "Hey, come on in," she suggested and closed the door. "Can I get you guys anything?"

"I'd like some juice, please," Trey said, and they went into the kitchen.

"Well, Trey, I've been away for a little while, and I'm not sure if I have juice, so let's check," she said and opened the pantry. She was relieved to see some apple juice on the shelf. She checked the date. It hadn't expired. She opened four cabinets before she finally found the cups and glasses.

"Are you okay?" Miles asked taking the cup from her hand and getting his son some ice for his juice.

"I'm fine, just jet lag, I guess," she said trying not to stare at him. He was fine as hell, and the photos of him didn't do him justice. If she was in Georgia, a man that looked like him wouldn't look at her twice on the street.

"Are you sure, because you seem different," he said, and she got nervous.

"Different, how?" she asked wondering if he could tell she wasn't Juliana.

"I don't know, not different bad—just different," he said and gave Trey the cup.

"Trey, come on, baby, and sit here with your juice and be careful," she said and helped him onto the stool at the island.

"See, like that," he said amazed.

"Like what, Miles?" she asked him.

"You know what, never mind. I'm just so happy to see you, babe. I've missed you so much," he said pulling her close again, and it felt odd. He was a stranger to her, and she didn't know how she was going to be able to be physical with him, because he was definitely interested in some physical contact with her. He tried to hold her and kiss her, but she only gave him a couple of pecks and moved to the fridge.

"So are you guys hungry?"

"Yea, where do you wanna go?" Miles asked because Juliana never cooked.

"Well, I've been eating fast food and takeout for the last ten weeks. I'd like to make something," she said, and Miles almost hit the floor.

"You cook? Please, Jules, your pots and pans are still brand-new."

"Well, maybe it's time I break them in," she said going through her sister's cabinets trying to see what she had to work with. She looked through her spices and grabbed the pad and pen from the fridge to make a list of what she needed. She called the guesthouse and sent Rocky to the store to get the items on the list.

Then she and Miles sat in the family room while Trey played video games in the media room and they talked. Miles was not only smart and talented he was interesting. She talked to him and felt comfortable with him, and she could tell he adored Juliana. Just the way he touched her and the way he was with her, and she wondered how Juliana went for an evil man like Reg when she had a sweetheart like Miles.

When Rocky finally made it back with the groceries Julia got started. She cooked a roast, cabbage, potatoes, and corn bread. A meal most people in Cali hardly ate, but she missed eating a good home cooked meal. They sat at the table to eat, and Miles and Trey grabbed their forks and began to dig in.

"Wait, hold on, you guys. Grace—hello?" she said reaching for their hands, and they stared at her. "Give me your hands, please. We don't enjoy our blessings without giving thanks to God for them," she said. Amazed, Miles and Trey gave her their hands, and she said grace.

"Jules, when did you start saying grace?" Miles asked, and she forgot who she was supposed to be.

"I always say grace," she said grabbing her fork.

"Juliana, you do not," he said, and the name Juliana penetrated her ears.

"Okay, Miles, I started at my aunt's, okay?" she said and took a bite of her food.

"Wow, Jules, this is good. I never knew you could cook like this," Miles said licking his fingers.

"Well, my dear, there's a lot you don't know about me," she said and smiled. After dinner she cleaned, and Miles kept her company in the kitchen. He went over to the bar and made them both a drink, and he handed her one.

"What's this?" she asked and took a sip and frowned.

"It's an apple martini. You love these," he said wondering what has gotten into her.

"Aw, I'm sorry. Just haven't had one in a while," she said lying again.

"Well, I'd love to meet your aunt. To meet someone who can tell you what to do, I'd like to shake her hand," he said and took a sip of his drink.

"I didn't think I was that bad," she said taking another sip. It was pretty good. She thought about the night Juliana had made her, her first drink and she tried hard not to get teary-eyed. She took another swallow hoping maybe the drink would help calm her nerves.

"Yea, baby, you've been pretty much a bitch since I've known you, and I know you may not try to be, but you are."

"Well, I have changed a little, I guess. Being around family does that to you," she said and took another sip.

"So how is your aunt?" he asked.

"Dead," she said, and the tears formed. She needed a reason to grieve more for Juliana, and that helped her to be able to cry without question.

"Dead? Aw, baby, I'm so sorry," he said and hugged her, and she cried some more.

"I hadn't seen her since I was eighteen, and I forgot how close we were, and for her to die after me being there for one day," she cried, and he held her.

"Wow, baby, that must have been hard. You should have called me. I would have been there for you. I mean, why did you stay so long?"

"I didn't plan on it, and being there with complete strangers was hard, but I had to do a few things for her just to make sure the rest of the family would be okay, so that's why I stayed," she said thinking about how she spent ten weeks learning everything that was needed to know about Juliana so she could make sure her family stayed safe.

"Well, in the future, if you ever have something hard or difficult to deal with, let me know so I can be there for you. I care for you a great deal, and I'm here to help you in whatever it is," he said, and she wanted so badly to mouth the words "help me," but she didn't know if the camera could see her lips moving.

"I know, Miles, and you are the only one I'll ever call on if I need help with anything," she said feeling safe for a change. She didn't want him to leave because she felt like he was the only one that could help her that was not on Reg's side. She finished her drink, and he made her another. They sat on the sofa and continued to talk.

"So are you ready to get back to work? I have this song that I wrote that I'm dying to get you in the studio to record."

"You wrote me a song, Miles?" she asked forgetting again.

"Yea, that's what I do, Juliana."

"I know, I'm just saying you are always focusing on writing for me, and you should concentrate on other artists," she said trying to cover what she asked him like an idiot.

"I do, Jules, but your voice is so beautiful, and when I'm writing, I imagine what you'll sound like singing it."

"Well, I can't wait to hear it," she said and took another sip of her drink. Now she was starting to feel it.

"How about you come by tomorrow morning and we'll take a stab at it and see what we can do with it?" he said and finished his drink.

"Okay, that sounds good," she agreed and finished hers and put her glass down. He sat there and stared at her. "What?"

"I can't put my finger on it, but you just seem different, Jules. I mean, your presence is so much warmer, not like before."

"Well, Miles, death can make you see things in a different light. To lose a loved one is a way to transform someone into someone new," she said and tried not to tear up. If it wasn't for her sister's death she wouldn't be pretending to be someone she was not.

"I guess," he said.

"Believe me, it cuts like a knife," she told him, and he took her hand.

"Well, I gotta go and get Trey home into bed," he said standing, and she didn't want him to go. She was scared to be there alone because Reg had a key and the code to her gate, and she was scared he'd just show up anytime.

"Already?" she asked standing, hoping he'd stay longer.

"Well, if I didn't have Trey with me, baby, you know I'd stay because I want some of this," he said pulling her close, and the liquor made her kiss him back passionately. She didn't know how, but her nipples became erect so she pushed him away and started praying for God to forgive her. She was not a fornicator and she still had not given her body to a man.

"Well, I'll be over in the morning so we can work on that song," she said and gave him a warm smile.

"Okay, baby, I'll see you then," he said and went to get Trey. He was on the sofa in the media room sleeping so Miles picked him up. Julia walked them to the door, and Miles leaned in and gave her another sweet kiss, and she hated herself for liking it. He had been with her sister, and she had no idea how she was going to keep him off of her. She thought about breaking up with him, but she didn't know anyone else in L.A. He was her only hope. When she locked the door her phone rang. It was Reg.

"Good job, Julia, you did well."

"I'm not doing this for you. I'm doing this for my family," she spat.

"That's quite all right, Julia, that's fine. I can't argue with that. You just keep up the good work and everyone will be happy. Oh, and in the morning, don't leave that house to go to Miles until I get there. I got something for you. Sleep tight," he said and hung up.

She was nervous, but at least she felt better that he wouldn't be coming over until the morning. She went to shower and looked around and didn't find a camera in the bathroom. She checked as thoroughly as she could and thanked God he'd at least give her that privacy. She got into bed and prayed before going to sleep. She lay there and couldn't help the tears for her sister that fell. She was kind of glad she was there because if she was not, she and her family may not have known about Reg and what he did. She just had to figure out some way to shut Reg down.

Chapter Seven

THE NEXT morning when Julia got up she was shaking from the bad dream she had. She dreamt about her sister being on stage singing and someone shot her from the audience and in her dream there was so much blood. She ran on the stage and tried to keep her sister alive by putting pressure on her wound, but she couldn't stop the bleeding. She woke up in tears and wondered how she was going to make it with her sister being dead.

How could she be dead, just gone, and she wouldn't be able to see her again? She wiped her eyes and looked at the clock. It was eight A.M. She went to the bathroom and sat there for a few moments and tried to get herself together. She gave herself a headache trying to figure out how to get help without being caught by Reg. She wondered how she was going to break away without Reg hurting another one of her family members.

After she washed her face and brushed her teeth, she headed downstairs and made herself some breakfast. Once she ate, she opened the front door and looked around and wondered how Reg would know if she just walked off the property and went to a neighbor's, but she looked up and noticed the cameras posted on the outside of her sister's home, so she went back inside. "Lord, what am I going to do?" she said out loud. She went back upstairs and went through her sister's closet to find something to wear. All of her sister's clothes were sexy, tight, and too revealing for her taste, but she had no choice. She took another shower and got dressed. Then she went into the kitchen and turned on the television. That's when she heard the door open.

She got up and went into the great room, and, of course, there stood Reg. She was not happy to see his evil ass.

"Good morning," he said, and she just looked at him. "How was your first night home?" he asked with a smile.

"My home is in Georgia," she said, and he laughed.

"Look, Julia, don't start . . . it's too early in the morning, okay?" he said moving over to the kitchen island. "I brought something for you," he said and laid his briefcase on the island and opened it.

"What is it, a poisonous apple?" she asked being smart.

"Nope, but that's a good idea. In case I need to send one to Janice, Jessica, or Jada," he said naming her three sisters. "I got a little device that you need to put in your purse, along with your tracking device," he said bringing a foreign-looking object over to her. "This is so I can hear everything you say," he said putting it in her hand. "I have to make sure you don't go over to Miles's place and spill the beans."

"Okay, so you don't trust me?"

"No, I don't. I trusted your sister, but she disappointed me," he said and went back over to his briefcase.

"What exactly did my sister do, Reg?"

"You don't need to worry about that. You just need to go over to Miles like you planned and make sure I can hear you at all times. As I told you before . . . if at any point I can't reach you, I will make a call and somebody in Georgia is going to be visited, and trust, it will look like an accident. We don't want anyone to die in a freak accident, do we?" he said with a grim look in his eyes. He knew Julia was terrified of him. He had no intentions on harming her family, but that was the only way he could keep her in check.

"So, Reg, how long is this charade going to go on?"

"As long as I say, now have a good day," he said and left. Julia put the little device that he gave her in her purse, and then she called Buster to take her to Miles's place. By the time they arrived she was totally nervous. She knew how to mimic Juliana, but her voice was a little stronger, and she was afraid she'd mess up and blow her cover. She got out of the car and walked up to the door, and Miles opened the door before she could ring the bell.

"Hey, baby, you're here early," he said and kissed her.

"You said in the morning," she replied and walked in.

"Well, your mornings are usually after two in the afternoon."

"Well, I'm here," she said, and he kissed her again.

"So do you want something to drink?"

"Yea, some iced tea," she replied looking around trying to take it all in because she wasn't familiar with his house.

"Okay, a Long Island Iced Tea coming right up," he said, and she stopped him.

"No, Miles, just an iced tea."

"When did you start drinking iced tea without driving it through Long Island?" he asked.

"In New York," she said lying.

"Well, I don't have any iced tea. Normally, you'd want a shot of something before you learn a new song."

"It's a bit early," she said looking around.

"Okay, but that is strange. I've known you to drink as early as seven A.M. if you were up."

"Well, I'm glad I don't feel like that anymore," she stated and went over to the window to check out the view. "So where is this song?" she said turning around to face him because he was close to her.

"Here at the piano," he said and she followed him over. She put her handbag on a little table close to the piano because she wanted to make sure Reg could hear her at all times. She picked up the sheet music and looked over it. It was good, and she could see he was a great song writer. "Now, I will run through the words once, and then you see how it feels," he said, and she sat with him on the bench and he went through the first verse and by the second verse she had the feel of it. She hummed the words and put the sheet back on the piano. Once he finished, she took a go at it and began to play it, and Miles almost fell off the bench. "Hold on, hold on," he said, and she stopped immediately.

"What?" she asked confused.

"When did you start reading music?" he asked, and she paused. She forgot that Juliana couldn't read music. She could play by ear, but she never learned to read music.

"I have a confession," she said and looked away.

"What's that?" he asked wondering how she was going to explain this one.

"I've been taking music lessons, okay? But please don't say anything. I was too embarrassed to say that I've been taking lessons," she said.

"Hey, why would you be embarrassed? That's a good thing, baby. I'm glad you did that, but you know you could have come to me if you wanted lessons. I would have helped you," he said touching her hand softly, and she had to get up. He was such a sweet man, and to be around him made Julia feel feelings she had never felt before around a man.

"I know, but I wanted to do it on my own," she replied posting herself next to the piano. "How about you give me the lyrics and you play," she suggested with a smile.

"Okay," he said and handed her the music sheet.

They ran through it a few times, and it didn't take her long before she had it. He began to play again from the top, and she closed her eyes and listened to the melody of the song. She looked at the lyrics and began to sing, and Miles looked at her like she was a stranger. Her voice sounded so fresh and renewed, that he thought the time off did her well.

He played and was mesmerized by her voice. It was smoother than it was before, and he wondered if it was because she hadn't had a drink in the ten weeks she was away, because she nailed it.

"Damn, baby, you were amazing. We need to record this song today," he said, and she couldn't believe he enjoyed her singing as much as Juliana's. She knew she could sing well, but Jules was the star . . . she was the professional.

"Really? You think so?" she asked and blushed a little.

"Oh yea, you smashed it, baby, and I don't know what happened to your voice in the past few weeks, but Reg is going to flip when he hears this song," he said gathering the music sheets. The name Reg made her smile fade, and he realized it. "Baby—are you okay?" he asked.

"Yes, I'm fine," she said giving him a fake smile.

"Well, I'll tell you what. I got to go to Trey's game at one so maybe meet me at the studio at four," he said putting his arms around her. She didn't have anything to do, and she didn't want to leave Miles.

"Well, I want to stay with you. I would love to go to Trey's game," she said. Miles thought he was dreaming.

"Are you serious? I thought you never wanted to go to one of his boring little pee-wee games," he stated, repeating what Juliana said once before to him.

"No, I want to, and I want to hang out with you today, if that's okay," she asked, and his dick got hard. He was ready to take her into his bedroom until game time.

"Cool, I want to see you naked anyway," he said, and he kissed her passionately, and she had to stop him. She did like him, but she was not ready for intimacy with him. She was too afraid to give him her body, even if she was ready. She barely knew him, and having sex with him was the last thing she wanted to do.

"Hey, baby—relax, we have plenty of time for that," she said trying to cool the situation.

"But, Jules, it's been a long time, and I miss your body," he said kissing her again, and by now, her body screamed. She never wanted a man like that in her life, and she was tempted to let him do her, but the image of her father in the pulpit popped in her head.

"I know, Miles, but Trey is here, and I don't want him to hear us making love. I'll take care of you later. I promise," she said.

"What's with you?" he asked wondering why she was putting him off. Trey's room was nowhere near his room, and Trey being there never stopped her from serving him up before. It's been a long while since they had sex, and he wasn't seeing anyone else, so he was about to go crazy.

"What do you mean, Miles?"

"You act as if you didn't miss me," he said with a sad look on his face.

"I did miss you, Miles, I've just had a lot on my mind, and I just don't know . . . you know?" she said and looked at him in the eyes. "But I did miss you," she said touching his face gently trying to make him feel at ease. He was so kind, and she liked him and really wished she could just tell him the truth. She wanted to tell him she was a fraud, but she knew the device in her purse was listening to every word she was saying.

"I know, Jules, but, babe, it's been a whole minute," he said pulling her closer to him again and that scared Julia to death.

"Listen, Miles, I'll take care of you soon, okay? Just give me a minute to regroup," she asked, and Miles gave up. He wasn't happy, but he was a gentleman.

"Okay, babe, but know that I want you, and I can't wait to have you again," he said and kissed her.

"I know, baby, me too," she said and gave him a warm smile.

Chapter Eight

"GO, TREY, go!" Julia yelled cheering in the stands at Trey's Little League baseball game, and once again, Miles was blown away. Not only did she go to Trey's game with him, but she was in the stands cheering and having a good time. She ate two hot dogs, and she never ate hot dogs or junk food. She put her finger in her mouth and whistled loud. Miles was happy that she was finally enjoying an afternoon out at one of his son's games.

"I see you're enjoying yourself," he commented.

"Yeah, I am, and Trey is good. He can go pro," she said and whistled again.

"I've asked you a million times to come to one of Trey's games, and now you see what you've been missing. I remember you saying, 'I'm not sitting on them filthy bleachers in the hot sun to watch a bunch of little brats play ball,'" he said mimicking the real Juliana.

"Well, all that has changed. If I'm free I will never miss another game," she promised and jumped up and cheered for Trey as he slid into home base and scored the team's first point. "Yes! Yes!" she yelled clapping and whistling. She was impressed to see such a little guy play so well.

When the game was over they headed to the studio. They were in Miles's SUV, and Trey was talking to his dad nonstop, and Julia just smiled and watched them carry on with their father-son conversation.

"Wow, Trey, man, you played an awesome game, dude. I didn't know you had skills like that," Julia said trying to get in on their conversation.

"That's because you've never come to any of my games . . . duh," he said and turned his attention back to his dad, and Julia felt awkward. She wondered how Juliana really treated Trey because he didn't like her much at all.

"Well, that's because I was busy a lot, but from now on if I'm free I'll be at all of your games."

"Yeah, sure," he said, and Julia was puzzled.

"Hey, young man, watch your mouth. Now, Juliana says she'll come, and that means she'll come," Miles said.

"Dad, she always says she is going to do things with me, but she never does. She is always mean to me, and she hates baseball," he said, and he sat back in the seat with his arms folded across his chest.

"Well, Trey, I'm sorry, sweetie, and I am going to keep my word from now on, okay? I don't hate baseball, and I am so sorry for ever being mean to you, I really am. Can I have another chance? I promise I'll do exactly what I say I'll do, and I will never make you feel the way I used to make you feel, Trey. I'm sorry, okay? I will be better, I promise. Deal?" she said and turned around in her seat and held out her hand to shake. He was hesitant, but he gave in.

"Deal," he said smiling. He could tell Juliana was different too, not the evil witch that she used to be. She was never nice to him, but he decided he'd give her another chance, because she did seem nicer. Miles was happy and glad she took her trip to New York because everything about her was better, he thought as he parked. When they got upstairs into the studio, Reg barged in the door and demanded Julia to follow him to his office, and Miles wondered what he was so mad about.

He was usually sweet to Juliana, and Miles thought at times that he was having an affair with her, but he knew Lisa would castrate him if he got caught messing around, especially with Juliana. She never verbalized it, but Miles knew she was jealous of Juliana the way she snarled and gave her the evil eye every time they were in the same room.

Julia walked fast trying to keep up with Reg as she followed him down the hall to his office. There were beautiful pictures of her sister all over the building, and she wondered how she passed for such a diva like Juliana. When she walked in behind him, he slammed the door and it made her jump and her heart raced. She wondered if he was going to choke the life out of her the way he looked at her.

"Okay, change of plans. I heard you singing this morning at Miles's, and you did not take it light. You sounded like Juliana, but then you didn't. We are going in an entirely different direction with your new CD. Your voice has a little extra something that Juliana didn't have, and I know you know how to mimic her, but I wanna go with that extra jazz you carry."

"So what do you want me to do, Reg? Sing like Juliana or sing like me?" she asked confused.

"You have to take it light on a few tracks. Mimic her on some, but we are going to switch it up a bit. I'm going to get another coach in L.A. to work with you, because Austin would see right through you. We are going to have to ease into this strong voice of yours. I mean, you sound like Juliana on some of your notes, but then you go further than she was able to go, and we have to work that in slowly," he said walking back and forth. He was thinking how he was going to pull off this change in the sound of her voice.

"I can sing like Jules, Reg. I can control my tempo," she said with her eyes watering because she wanted to do whatever he wanted to keep him under control. She was trembling because Reg terrified her, and if she had to mimic Juliana she would because she didn't want to see anyone else hurt. She didn't want to end up like her sister . . . dead and God knows where.

"You have to control it some, Julia, okay? You can't go in there tearing the house down. You cannot mess this up, you understand," he said moving closer to her. "No one can know that you're not her, okay? I swear if I go down someone is going to be hurt, so you have to do Juliana with a flare, so go in that studio and take it easy on some notes and don't hit notes you know Juliana couldn't hit, but give it a bit of your own style, because it works.

"Miles knows that your voice has gotten better and that was clever when you told him about secretly taking music lessons when you played for him. You just need to slow down until we get a vocal coach in here, and you will see the new coach each day while we're recording this CD.

"You sound phenomenal, that I can't take away from you, but you have to remember you are Juliana Valentine," he said, and she wiped her eyes. "And you are going to have to cut out all of this fucking crying, you got that? Juliana was never one to cry about anything, so cut it out!" he yelled, and she nodded.

"Now get back in there and make it light for this track. Don't hit no notes that you know Juliana was never able to hit," he said again, opening his jacket and showing her he had his gun with him. Her heart raced, and she wished she was in Georgia around friends and family and people she knew. That way she would not have been so afraid.

"Okay, Reg, I hear you, okay? I understand just please—," she tried to say, but there was a knock on the door. She straightened up, and Reg backed up out of her face.

She wiped her face one more good time, and then Reg said, "Come in."

"Hey, you two, what's going on? We need to get started," Miles said. He noticed the sad look on Julia's face, and he could tell she had been crying. "Jules, babe, what's wrong?"

"Aw, she's all right. I was just breaking the news to her about bringing on a new vocal trainer to help her out and you know Jules, she ain't tryin' to hear nothing nobody tells her. You know how stubborn this woman is," Reg said. Miles could tell there was more to it, but he didn't say anything.

"Well, I don't know, Reg. Austin has been her coach for years, and she sounded great this morning. You know, fresher, stronger. I don't know why she's been holding back, but this song we worked on this morning she nailed it," he said, and she gave him a faint smile. She was starting to like Miles and felt close to him, and she knew that he did care for her, or he cared for Juliana anyway.

"Oh yeah, let's hear it," Reg said, and they headed back into the studio. Julia had never been in a studio before—she just tried to remember everything Reg had taught her in her Juliana 101 lessons.

"Okay, Jules, we're going to run through this a few times before we actually record," Miles said and handed her a copy of the lyrics. Reg stood to the side giving Julia the evil eye, and she knew he meant business. She was okay because she could mimic Juliana in a heartbeat, and singing like her wasn't hard for her to do. Miles started playing and she made a mental note to keep it light, and she then started to sing. She controlled her vocals, but her style was a little smoother than Juliana's and that she couldn't change.

Reg bobbed his head and wished he had signed Julia in the first place instead of Juliana and maybe he wouldn't have been in his predicament. Julia was more humble, and Reg didn't like the method he had to use to keep her in line, but he knew without fear she'd tried something funny and he didn't want to be caught. He wasn't about to lose everything, nor was he going to prison. He wanted to make sure she wouldn't talk, and if fear was the motivation that was the tactic he was going to continue to use.

By the end of the song, the couple spectators in the room applauded. Most everyone that worked in the building enjoyed hearing Juliana sing and always found a way to sit in when she recorded. Julia sounded like Juliana, with a twist, and Miles wanted to record the song right away.

"So what 'cha think, Reg? Should we record this right away?" he asked. Reg was not enthusiastic like Miles thought he would be. Juliana sounded better than ever before, and now Reg was acting like she was a backup singer.

"No . . . we need to hold off and work on it a bit. I wanna get her working with someone else first. I mean, Austin is a great coach, but I think we should bring in somebody new, and then we can talk about recording this song and rerecording the other tracks," he said because he knew Austin would figure it out quicker than anyone, and Julia had to learn the other songs that they had already recorded.

"Reg, man did you not hear what I just heard? It was perfect, and Jules doesn't need a new coach—Austin Avery is the best," he said and gave Julia a warm smile.

"My company, my artist, my decision, and I say we are replacing Austin. Her voice doesn't need work, Miles—that I know. Austin just hasn't been pushing her to her full potential as you can clearly see, and that is what I plan to do by bringing on someone else. I say put this on hold for at least a couple weeks," he said, and Miles wondered what in the hell was going on. He was never like that when it came to Juliana, and she has recorded songs that Miles thought were not for her that Reg loved, and now they had the perfect song with the perfect sound and he was criticizing her efforts.

"Reg, Jules just smoked this song. I say we record," Miles suggested and Julia blushed. He really liked her singing, and that made her smile.

"And I say we wait!" Reg replied, raising his voice. "And, Jules, I expect to see you at eight A.M. to meet with Keith Moore. He wrote a song that I may want to put on this album, and I want to see if it works. I expect you to be on time, so don't go home and drink all night. Be ready to work!" he barked and walked out.

"What's with him, Jules? What happened in his office?" he asked, and she noticed her purse was on the other side of the glass, but there were a couple others around and she didn't know who she could trust so she didn't chance it.

"I don't know what he's so uptight about," she said and blew it off.

"Are you sure? You can tell me if something is wrong, babe. I got your back," he said grabbing her hands, and she smiled.

"Oh, you got my back?" she asked feeling safe with him.

"Oh, yes," he said and kissed her. "Are you ready to head out?" he asked.

"Yes, I have to get my purse, and we can go."

"So where do you want to go for dinner?"

"Well, I was going to cook. I left a list for Rocky to get some items from the grocery store for me, so I was thinking some grilled chicken breast. I can throw them on the grill with some steamed veggies," she said, and he tilted his head and touched her forehead.

"Who are you, and what did you do to my Jules?" he asked, and she wanted to say, "I didn't do anything, but Reg did."

"Nothing, the weather is so nice today, and I figured I should get out and light up the grill. It's never been used so I figured tonight will be a perfect night to use it."

"Okay, I'm game if it's going to be as good as the meal you cooked last night . . . I'm there," he said and kissed her again, and she liked it. She liked the attention and wondered if he'd be this attentive or even like her if she was just plain old Julia and not glamorous Juliana.

"Okay, let me get my purse and we can go," she said.

"Right, I'll get Trey from upstairs and take him home, and you and I can go grill."

"No, he can come; he needs to eat too," she smiled.

"You want Trey to come?" he asked thinking she had to be on drugs.

"Yes, I would like for him to come. We can stop and get him some bedclothes. He can take his bath, and we can watch some TV," she suggested. She knew Reg would be watching, but she also knew Reg wouldn't bother her if Miles was around, and he probably wouldn't shoot anyone with a kid there. Before they made their exit, Summer, a familiar face walked in, but Julia had to think, for a moment what her name was.

"Jules welcome back love," she said and hugged her.

"It's good to be back," Julia said and it hit her. It was her personal assistant. She only had brief conversations with her over the phone and by email, when Juliana was supposed to be in New York. Julia completely forgot she was stopping by the studio that evening to bring her up to date on some upcoming events and appointments.

"Hey Miles, I know you're glad to have this woman back," she said smiling at him.

"Yes, she's been away too long," he said.

"Well I won't keep you guys long. I just stopped by to bring Jules up to date on some things," Summer said. Miles nodded and decided to go and get Trey.

"Summer please make it quick, because I gotta run," Julia instructed giving her *Juliana* attitude.

"Of course," she said and laid her planner on the piano and flipped through. "Okay tomorrow you have a two o'clock interview with *Vibe*, so I'll have Kev come over for your wardrobe and Rob will meet up with you for your hair and makeup," she said quickly and scrolled down. "And then Wednesday you have a charity event for breast cancer and then you are free for a week and I will shoot you an email with what's next."

"Okay that sounds great Summer and thank you for dropping by," she said. Summer smiled and nodded and closed her planner.

"No problem. I will see you tomorrow and you have a nice night Jules," she said and hurried out. Miles came back with Trey and they were all set and they ran into Reg when they got off the elevator. The last face Julia wanted to see.

"Eight sharp," he spat. She rolled her eyes. Reg was the one who put her in her sister's shoes, and she absolutely despised him.

Chapter Nine

DINNER WAS delicious, and Miles and Trey were speechless after their meal. They were both wondering how Juliana learned to cook so well when she never boiled water for them before. They were so pleased with the meal they both asked for seconds, and that's what Julia loved—for folks to enjoy her cooking, like her family back home. There was never a Sunday that she and her sisters did not cook up a huge meal, and she was glad to see Miles and Trey cleaning their plates.

She cleared the patio table, and Miles went to refill their glasses with wine. She was never a drinker, but the Riesling he got out of the wine cooler was a perfect choice for her introduction to wine. They sat at the patio table and played Uno for a while until it was time for Trey to take a bath.

They went inside, and Julia went into maternal mode and ran Trey's water and picked up his clothes from the floor and put them into the laundry bag. She poured more bubble bath in the tub and told him she'd be right back to turn off the water. Miles offered to do it, but she told him to have a seat and relax, and he did just that. He was a single dad, and although he had a nanny, he did mostly everything for his own son. When Julia went back into the bathroom to turn off the water she told Trey to make sure he washed behind his ears and inside of his belly button, and he laughed.

"Why do I have to wash inside of my belly button?" he asked giggling.

"Because if you don't, little nasty germs will live in there and cause you to have a stinky belly button, and if you have a stinky belly button your clothes are going to run away because they don't want to be on a little boy with a stinky belly button," she said making faces, and he laughed louder.

"Do you wash inside of your belly button, Juliana?" he asked and she wished they knew her as Julia and not as Juliana.

"Yes, I do, every single day," she said and put bubbles on his nose. "Now you finish up in here and make sure you don't miss a spot, okay?" she said standing.

"Okay," he said and grabbed the fancy sponge. Everything in Juliana's home was made for girls so he had to bath in lavender bubble bath and use an expensive sponge to bathe with. She left him and went into the room and took his pajamas from his overnight bag and laid them on the bed.

Since her luggage and all of her items were gone from that room she went down the hall to Juliana's room and got some lotion for Trey and came back and got him out of the tub.

"I can put lotion on by myself," he said with his towel around his little waist, being a big boy.

"Oh, okay," Julia said and handed it to him. He asked her to turn her head while he put on his little boxers.

"You can turn around now," he said, and she smiled. "This lotion smells like girl lotion," he said rubbing it on his arms.

"I know, sweetie, but all I have is girl stuff," she said helping him rub it in.

"Well, I'm going to have to bring my own the next time, because I don't wanna smell like a girl," he said making faces.

"No problem . . . I'll be sure to have Buster go out and get you your own lotion, bath sponge, and bubble bath for boys tomorrow, and I'm going to put it in the bathroom for you so the next time you spend the night it will already be here, okay?" she said holding his pajama pants and he stepped in.

"Miss Juliana, why are you so nice now? Did a fairy princess put you under a spell?" he asked, and she laughed.

"Well, Trey, sometimes people are mean because they are not happy, and for a long time, Miss Juliana wasn't happy, and now Miss Juliana has a new start on life, so she's decided to be nicer to the ones that she cares about."

"I know you like my dad, but when did you start liking me?" he asked, and she was surprised.

"Listen, Trey, I'm sorry for the way the old Juliana treated you and how she made you feel, okay, but I like you, sweetie, I was just too unhappy about other things before and I let it get in the way of how I treated others, but I promise you that you and I are going to be buddies now," she said, and he gave her a hug. "Now come on, it's bedtime," she announced, and he climbed in. "Close your eyes and say your prayers," she said, and he looked at her strange.

"What are prayers?" he asked, and she almost fell to the floor. No way did this kid not know what prayers were. She knew she was going to have to talk to Miles about that for sure.

"Well, it's when you talk to God and tell him thanks for things, and you ask him for things you want," she said trying to keep it simple.

"Like if I want to steal second base, I can ask God?" he asked, and she smiled.

"Sure, exactly . . . now, I'm going to give you the basics to start with, and after you learn the Lord's Prayer you'll find yourself praying all the time."

"Okay," he said and went with it.

"Now close your eyes," she told him, and he did. "Don't fall asleep before we finish because God doesn't like that," she said, and he laughed. She began, and before they were done, Miles was standing in the doorway. "Amen," she said and pulled up the covers. "Now I'm going to get your dad so he can say good night."

"No, I'm here," he said surprising her.

"How long have you been there?" she asked hoping he wouldn't be upset about teaching his son how to pray.

"Not long," he replied and walked over to the bed. "Good night, son, I'll see you in the morning."

"Night, Dad," he said, and Miles kissed him on the forehead. He closed his eyes, and they turned to leave. "Juliana, can I have a kiss?" Trey asked her, and she felt warmhearted.

"Sure," she answered and went over to him. She leaned in and kissed his cheek, and he instantly blushed. "Good night, sweetie," she said and tucked him tighter.

"Good night," he yawned. He was asleep before they made it to the bottom of the steps.

They went back outside on the patio and sat by the pool. Both were silent for a while, then she asked him, "Miles, have you ever taken your son to church?"

"No, and while we are on that subject, when did you become so spiritual?"

"Well, Miles, I have been this way all my life; just got beside myself and lost touch of who I was and where I come from," she said looking away and wondered how Juliana strayed so far away from God. She felt sorry for her sister's soul at that point and hoped she made amends with God before her demise weeks ago.

"I've never taken him to church. Don't know why . . . I guess you can say the same about me. I've been away from my family for so long, and my daddy was a minister," he said, and she wanted so badly to tell him about her daddy being a minister too, but she couldn't.

"Really?" she said shocked.

"Yep, I grew up in the church, and music was my life, and my daddy didn't want to see me living the lifestyle of a R&B, pop, or secular artist, so when I left I never went back and my dad died when Trey was four. The first time he met his granddad he was in a casket," Miles said and took a sip of his drink.

"Miles, I'm so sorry to hear that," she said and reached over and touched his hand. He held her hand, and they sat in silence for a few moments. "It's such a beautiful night," she said, and he agreed. It was so peaceful out there, and she wished she was with him as herself and not as her sister so she could tell him about her, her life, and her past, but she couldn't open up because she didn't know anything about Juliana anymore, not like she thought she did. She knew Jules had a good heart beneath the evil exterior that everyone knew her as, but she wished they all knew the Juliana from Georgia, with four sisters and a preacher for a daddy.

"Yes, tonight feels good," he said and looked at her, and she knew he wanted her. She wanted him too and only imagined what it would be like making love. She had boyfriends, and she had kissed men before, but she was saving herself for marriage, but now she was thinking otherwise. He was so gentle and sweet, and she never enjoyed a man as much as she enjoyed him. Her body burned for him to touch her. She didn't know how much longer she could hold out and not give into her flesh. Deep down she knew it was sinful, but she felt as if she had finally fallen for a man.

"Have you ever been in love?" she asked and sipped her wine.

"Yes, once," he said, and she wanted him to tell her more. "Trey's mother was my first love, and I'da done anything for that woman," he said. She was afraid to ask what happen because she didn't know if he and her sister had talked about her before, but her curiosity made her ask.

"What happened?" she asked nervously hoping he wouldn't give her the *you know what happened* look.

"Well, you remember Cara White?" he asked.

"Yea, I've heard a couple of her songs," she said knowing the artist, but she died of an overdose about nine or ten years ago.

"Well, we were married," he said, and her mouth dropped open.

"You were married to Cara White?" she asked astounded.

"Yes, that was Trey's mom. She overdosed when he was nine months," he said, and she wished Reg would have told her that.

"Wow, I can't believe it. I didn't know," she said hoping that was something Juliana really didn't know.

"Well, no one knows really. We lived out in New York then, and I moved out here a couple months after she died to start over. She was only twenty-three and at the beginning of her singing career," he said. Julia let the air out of her chest.

"Wow, Miles, I'm sorry. She had a beautiful voice, and I loved her music," she said remembering how her hairdresser used to play her CD to death. Julia was about seventeen or eighteen, and she remembered because that was around the time Juliana first left and the media talked about Cara's overdose more than they talked about Anna Nicole and her illegitimate child. Her daddy made a comment of how he never wanted that to happen to Juliana. That's one of the reasons she knew he hated her wanting to be an R&B artist.

"Yes, she did, and I wrote every song on her CD, and when it went platinum, she just lost control and let the life take over. She started partying and letting everybody pull her in different directions, and she was naïve and wouldn't listen to me when I told her that those were bad things for her. She'd tell me to stop trying to be her daddy. Next thing you know, I was home all the time with Trey. She started using and tried to hide it from me, but I knew. One day I was at the studio and the housekeeper walked in to find Trey screaming in his crib uncontrollably.

"His diaper was soaked, and when our housekeeper went to look for Cara, she was in her dressing room dead. She had been dead for five or six hours so she got up right after I left to use that mess and my son was in his crib all of those hours and I hated myself for leaving him when I knew his mother was a user," he said and took a few sips. Julia just sat there stunned.

"One thing I can say I respect about you. You drink—yea, like a fish, yes, but you despise drugs, and no matter who has offered or tried to turn you on, you are clean," he said, and Julia was relieved to hear that. She never imagined Juliana to get hooked on drugs, but she also never imagined her sister to stop praying to God either, so she was very relieved to hear that her sister was drug-free.

"Wow, Miles that is tragic. I can imagine that that had to be rough to lose her to drugs," she said, and he didn't say anything. "Since my aunt's death I see things differently, and I want to change, and I'm trying to be a better person," she said, and he could tell because she was definitely a better person.

"Yea, I know. It's like you have the same face, the same smile, the same body and scent, but your eyes are different because they are not so evil anymore. Your aura has changed, and in the last two days I feel closer to you than I ever felt in our entire relationship. You have taken our relationship to a new level since you've been back. I mean, with Trey and everything. I can't describe the way I'm feeling now," he said, and her heart raced. She felt the electricity and just knew that she was not going to be a virgin by morning.

"Miles, I know exactly how you feel. It's like I just met the man of my dreams, and I feel so good when I'm around you, and I want to be close to you every moment of the day," she said because she had fallen for him as if he was hers all along. She looked at him and blinked several times and asked God why things were happening that way. She couldn't understand how she wanted him the way she did and so soon. Maybe she fell in love with him after watching him on the DVDs Reg had her watching day in and day out.

She remembered thoughts of him vividly when Reg said, "This is Miles—your man, so you have to treat him as such." When she asked how was she supposed to be intimate with a stranger he asked her which was more important, her life or faking an orgasm? Her jaw dropped when he said it, but he was dead serious. So as she studied the DVDs, she paid close attention to his eyes and his lips and how he treated Juliana.

All in all, he was sexy at five feet ten inches tall. He was medium brown with soft eyes and long lashes that gave him an easy-to-talk-to look because he never looked angry in his eyes. He had a goatee with a small spot on each side that barely connected, but it wasn't noticeable to the eye at first glance. His lips were soft and had an even color, leaving evidence that he had never been someone to smoke. His shoulders were nice, chest was broad. Even though his stomach was not a six-pack, it didn't protrude at all and it wasn't fat; it was just not ripped.

He had a low faded haircut with traces of a soft gray, and even though Julia never asked, she knew he had her by six or seven years. He was warm and attentive, and he was so mellow. Even if she wanted to she couldn't help herself from wanting to be touched by this man.

He stood and reached for her hand, and she got up and followed him inside. She was trembling, but she followed him upstairs and wondered if this was going to be the moment that he figured out she wasn't Juliana. She didn't know how it was going to turn out, but she knew she wasn't going to turn back. They looked in on Trey, and then they headed to Juliana's bedroom. He closed the door softly, and she stood there nervous and afraid to move. He kissed her lips and could feel her shaking.

"What's wrong, baby?" he whispered.

"It feels like it's my first time," she said as if it was not, but it truthfully was.

"Don't worry, baby, I got you," he said and kissed her gently, making her feel as easy as he normally did. They slowly moved toward the bed, and he kissed her passionately as he undid the buttons on her blouse. She had on a black laced set from her sister's collection, and when he removed her top, he smiled, and now she was even more nervous. She wanted to go with the flow, but she was scared, and then she remembered the cameras.

"Wait, wait, wait, Miles, we can't," she said, and he stopped and was confused.

"What's wrong, Jules? Why are you torturing me like this?" he asked wondering what type of bullshit she was on.

"Listen, I want to, baby, I do. I want you so bad, but I can't tonight," she said nervously.

"Oh, I see what's going on," he said and stood and her heart started to pound. Had he figured her out? "I know what this is about," he said, and she wondered what he knew. Was he in on this with Reg?

"What, what is about?" she asked nervously.

"It's about you being afraid of getting pregnant?" he said, and she let out a deep breath.

"Well, I don't have any protection here," she said going with that. She honestly hadn't thought about that, but she was glad that's what he thought the problem was.

"Okay, baby, I do understand, and I'm not mad. I don't have anything with me either, so, hey . . . I'm cool," he said and gave her a soft peck.

"You sure you're okay?" she asked, and he smiled.

"Yea, I'm okay. I just wish you would get on some type of birth control, you know, for moments like this," he said and climbed into bed with her.

"I'll give that some serious thought," she said, and they lay there in their clothes. After a few moments of silence they were both asleep.

Chapter Ten

THE NEXT morning the ringing phone woke Julia up from her sleep. Miles was still sleeping, and the ringing phone didn't seem to bother him. She finally answered it after clearing her throat. She looked over at the clock and wondered who was calling her at six A.M.

"Hello," she said.

"Rise and shine, country girl, the car will be ready at seven thirty to take you to the studio," Reg said, and she wanted to hang up on him. She cringed at the sound of his voice and hated that she let him scare her into her predicament.

"Reg, it's six in the morning," she said and rubbed her face.

"I know, but you have to get up and be ready on time. You have songs to learn, and we don't have much time. Your new coach will drop in today, and you have a busy afternoon, so get up. It's time to work."

"Reg, I'm a quick study, so relax. Music is my life," she said moving to the edge of the bed because Reg's voice was loud and she didn't want Miles to overhear anything he said.

"I don't give a shit about that, Julia. I need to meet you so we can go through these tracks before everyone starts to pour in. I'm going to give you a copy of the recorded tracks, and you have to be ready to record them within a couple weeks, so this is urgent, so get your ass in gear.

"The car will be ready at seven thirty. Rob and Summer will be at the studio at noon to take you by *Vibe* and to get you prettied up for your interview. I'll have a couple notes written down for you just in case so you'll be fine. Once we are done, you'll be free to play with your boyfriend," he said, and she looked over at Miles. She couldn't wait for her day to be done so she could get back to him.

"Okay, Reg, I'll be ready," she said and hung up. She showered and when she came back into the bedroom Miles was still sleeping. She went into Juliana's dressing room and could not believe she had so many clothes and accessories to choose from. She opened up her sister's underwear drawer and found a cute bra and panty set and put it on. She put on some lotion and thought a moment on what to wear. She and Juliana wore the same size in clothes, but she just had slightly rounder hips and a tad bit more bottom. Their breasts were the same size, but Julia could use a few more sit-ups she thought even though her tummy was flat. She wasn't fat at all, but she knew Juliana was a little slimmer than she, maybe a few inches.

She walked back into the master bedroom in her undies because she still had not figured out what to wear. It's not because she didn't like any of her sister's clothes, she just didn't know what actually went with what. Before she could go back into the closet, Miles was up, and she froze because she only had on her panty and bra set.

"Good morning, sexy," he said and smiled.

"Miles," she said nervously. "Good morning," she said and stood there for a moment and knew it would be stupid to try to cover herself so she just imagined herself being in a bikini.

"You're up early," he said and stretched.

"Yea, I got to be ready by seven thirty. I have to be in the studio by eight o'clock to go over the tracks I've recorded to see what changes are going to be made and meet my new coach," she said and headed back into the closet. She didn't care what she picked out at that point; she just had to put on something and not prance around in front of Miles in her sexy underwear.

"Yea, well, I think it's silly Reg is bringing on someone new. I mean, you've worked with Austin ever since you signed with Tower Records. He knows Austin is like one of the best; that's why they brought him on for you."

"Well, Reg thinks he knows everything, so I'm not going to argue."

"I hear that. The only person that keeps his ass in check is his wife," he said, and Julia was shocked.

"His who?" she asked coming out of the closet.

"Lisa—she's the only one that he doesn't get away with his dumb shit," he said and went to the bathroom. Julia was confused. How was he married when all Juliana talked about was how they were going to be married? Why would Jules talk about marrying a man that was already married? She wondered if that was his motive for wanting her dead. Did she threaten to tell his wife or something? Why was she so in love with Reg and he was married, she wondered, as she stepped into a pair of slacks.

She grabbed a low-cut blouse and admired herself in the mirror when she looked at her reflection. Julia would have never worn a top that revealing or sexy, but since she was Juliana it was perfect. She went into a smaller room in the closet where

Juliana had a wall of jewelry. She had necklaces upon necklaces hanging on the jewelry wall and drawers and drawers of rings, bracelets, and other expensive accessories. Julia had so many choices she knew she couldn't go wrong if she tried.

When she was ready, she still had almost thirty minutes to spare so she put on an apron and made a quick breakfast for her, Miles, and Trey. Before the car came around someone walked in the kitchen door and she was wondering who in the hell the woman in the uniform was.

"Good morning, Miss Juliana, how are you today?" she said, and Julia guessed quickly that she was the housekeeper, but she had no idea what her name was.

"Good morning, I'm great. How are you?"

"Good and happy to be back. I thank you from the bottom of my heart for giving me a long paid vacation and for the ticket for me to go home to Puerto Rico to visit my family," she said, and Julia knew that was all Reggie's doing. She imagined he gave her a handsome amount to keep her away from the house for so many weeks. "And hello, little Trey," she said and squeezed Trey's cheeks.

"Hello, Miss Elsa," Trey said.

"Mr. Miles, how are you? It's so nice to see you again," she said being very friendly to everyone but Juliana. All Juliana got was a good morning and thanks for the paid vacation, but Trey and Miles got hugs and kisses.

"So, Elsa, how have you been?" Julia asked grateful Trey said her name.

"I'm fine, Miss Juliana, and don't worry, I'm going to get started right away."

"No hurry, Elsa . . . I'm leaving in a moment. Would you like some breakfast?" she asked, and Elsa's brow rose. Juliana has never been amiable. Elsa was scared to sit down.

"No, no, no, Miss Juliana, I'm fine. I'll hurry and get started," she said and went straight for the broom closet to get her apron and cleaning supplies.

"Now you are asking Elsa to sit and eat? After paying for her a ticket to go home and giving her time off with pay? I take what I said back last night. You must be on drugs."

"Huh?" she asked confused.

"That woman has worked for you for years and you've never offered her a glass of water. You told her she wasn't allowed to listen to Spanish music in this house while she cleans. Not only did you scare the crap out of her about Spanish music, you told her that headphones were not allowed when she was under your roof, and the only time you gave the poor woman a day off is on Christmas Day. Even when you're on tour, she comes and dusts and cleans to assure the house stays fresh and clean while you're gone," he said, and Julia was ashamed of Juliana. How could she deprive a person from music? The only way to clean is to some good music.

"Well, I feel differently now," she said and ran after Elsa. "Look, Elsa, I'm so sorry for before. You can listen to anything you want, as loud as you want. And headphones are allowed if that's what helps you make it through the day, and I'm so sorry for being mean or a bitch to you. I appreciate everything you do. It's because of you my life is easier because you keep this place looking beautiful, and from now on, when I'm on the road you only need to come once a week to keep down the dust, with double your regular pay, and holidays, you're off with pay," she said. Now the car was waiting for her. "Listen, I got to go, but eat, take your time, do what makes you comfortable, okay? Mi casa is su casa," she said and ran to get her purse. She kissed Miles and Trey good-bye and promised Miles she'd come by later.

Chapter Eleven

WHEN JULIA'S day was over she was exhausted. She didn't know how hard the life of a celebrity was until that day. She was pulled in every direction, and the photo shoot took forever because she had no clue what she was doing. Summer had to help her a lot and kept asking her if she was ill because she has done tons of photo shoots. Little did Summer know, it was her very first one.

Rob changed her hair four times total, and her face felt tender from taking off and reapplying makeup. She wanted to go home, but she told Miles and Trey that she'd come by when she was done working so she wanted to be a woman of her word.

When she made it to his house she remembered she had a gift for Trey, so she pulled out her cell phone to call Buster to bring the car back around. She wondered how he waited in the car for so many hours with nothing to do. She wondered what Reg was paying him for his silence.

She stood by the circular drive and waited for Buster to get the bag. She told him that she'd be a while and he was welcome to go anywhere he liked, but he said he'd be waiting for her no matter how long it took. She insisted on him going and assured him she wouldn't try any funny business.

"Trust me, Buster, I have too much to lose. So go and have some fun. I'll be right here with Miles. I'm not going anywhere," she said and winked. He nodded and put his finger over his lips and pointed to her purse, and she knew what he meant. The listening device in her purse was on and anything they said would have been heard.

"No, ma'am, I'll be right here in the car when you are ready," he said, and she smiled.

"Well, suit yourself. I'll call you when I want you to bring the car around," she said, and she winked again. "Enjoy your time alone in that boring car," she smiled, and he winked back at her as she headed back toward the door. She wondered how she could get Buster to break. He was different from Rocky, and Julia thought she may be able to bribe him with food. He was a big guy on the outside, but Julia would bet he was a teddy bear on the inside. She knew from then on she was going to make sure he ate whatever she cooked and she was going to be his friend if it meant helping her get free.

She rang Miles's doorbell. She was excited because she had an autographed baseball from Alex Rodriguez. He was at *Vibe* magazine that afternoon, and she made sure he autographed a ball for Trey. When Miles opened the door he was looking exceptionally handsome. He looked like he had a fresh haircut, and his beard was trimmed nicely. He smiled brightly and greeted her with a tight hug and soft kiss.

"Hello to you too," she said, and he let her come inside.

"Hey, I thought you'd never get here," he told her closing the door.

"Trust me, I thought the same thing. I had a very long day, and I'm beat," she said going over to the sofa where she took a seat. He went over and poured her a glass of wine, and she thanked him when he handed it to her. She needed to relax, and that was a good way for her to.

"So how was the interview?"

"It was good, actually. I was nervous at first, but it was easier than I thought it would be," she said not realizing what she was saying again.

"Jules, you nervous? Please. You've done millions of interviews, and you are a camera hog," he said joining her on the sofa.

"No, I'm not," she said and gently pushed his arm.

"You are too. Most people run from the paparazzi, but you run to them," he said causing her to laugh.

"Well, today was a little different, I guess. Wasn't like usual," she said trying to cover herself.

"Different how?" he asked and took a sip of his drink.

"I don't know, just different. By the way, that reminds me, I have a gift for Trey," she said picking up the little bag on the floor by her purse.

"Hold on . . . Trey!" he yelled. Trey ran out into the front.

"Yes, Dad?" he said, and then saw Julia.

"Juliana, when did you get here? I've been waiting for you all day," he said and hugged her neck.

"You were?" She was happy to see him too. "Guess what? I got something for you," she told him, and he was excited.

"What you bring me?" he asked, and she pulled the ball out of the bag. He looked at it strangely. He had a ton of baseballs.

"Wow, a baseball?" he said disappointed.

"No, Trey, this isn't just a baseball. It's an autographed ball to you from Alex Rodriguez," she said, and she almost passed out when he knew exactly who he was.

"Alex—as in the New York Yankees, third base man, Alex Rodriguez?" he asked with his eyes as wide as saucers.

"Yep," she answered.

"You went all the way to New York for me?"

"No . . . silly, he was here in California today, and I had to make sure he signed a ball for my little guy."

"Wow, thanks, Juliana, this is the best present ever," he exclaimed and ran back into his room, after planting a wet kiss on Julia's cheek.

"Wow, Jules that was nice of you to get that for him."

"No biggie," she smiled and took another sip, and she could feel it working already.

"So what did you do today?" she asked him.

"Nothing too much . . . I've been working on this song, but I just can't seem to get it the way I want it."

"Let me see it," she asked.

"Jules, you don't know anything about writing songs," he said and brushed her off.

"Yes, I do. I've written a ton of songs. Your songs are not the only songs I record. I had two CDs before you started writing for me," she said, and he laughed.

"What's funny?" she asked.

"What's funny is that none of your CDs went platinum 'til I started writing for you," he informed her matter-of-factly, and she laughed.

"Oh, so you got jokes," she said and took another sip.

"Yep, I got jokes. Listen, sit tight and let me go put Trey to bed," he said getting up.

"No, I'll come with you. He needs to learn how to say his prayers at night," she stated and put her drink down. They both went into Trey's room. After reciting his prayers they tucked him in and kissed him good night and that felt really nice to Julia. She imagined how good it will be when she is married and with kids. She knew she was going to be a great mom—if God allowed her to live to see it.

They were back on the sofa, and Miles reached over and grabbed her feet to remove her sandals. He massaged her feet as she laid her head back and enjoyed the massage. She continued to sip on her wine, and when she was done, he offered to refill her glass, and she didn't decline. Halfway through her second glass she was feeling warm and not from the temperature, but in other ways.

She looked at him, and he looked at her, and she didn't resist him when he leaned in to kiss her. He slowly moved his hand down to her breast, and her erect nipples wanted him to please them without her top and bra. The more they kissed the more excited she became. Tonight she wanted to give it to Miles. She wanted to give away her love for the first time to him, and she wasn't going to turn him down.

"Oh, baby, I missed you," he said between kisses. "Let me make love to you," he murmured, and she laid her head back and let him lick her neck and suck on her skin. He massaged her breasts, and it felt so good. He pulled her top over her head and exposed another pretty laced bra, but he didn't have time to admire it.

He lifted her bra, exposing her breasts, and her heart was pounding fast. His hot breath was over her left nipple and that made her hot spot go places and do things she couldn't remember it ever doing before. He moved to the right nipple and sucked it perfectly, and she wanted to do more. He took her hand and put it on his erection, and she didn't know what to do. She just held it, not sure what he wanted. He took her hand and moved it around, showing her what he wanted her to do, and she played it off like she knew what was going on.

"Come on," he said getting up and helping her off the sofa. He led her into his bedroom, and she tried to pretend that his room wasn't a foreign space. He pushed her back onto the bed, and she watched him remove his shirt and undo his pants.

'Oh, God, please, Jesus, help me,' she said in her mind when she saw his beautiful shoulders and tight chest. She was new at what was about to go down, but she figured she watched enough movies to make it. After he stepped out of his pants he went to undress her. When she was down to her panties, she was starting to feel a little more relaxed. His kisses were the reason for that.

He removed his boxers and she stared because she had never seen a grown man's dick before, not in person. He removed her panties and began to rub her between her legs, and she moaned loudly from him touching her spot. She had never been touched down there before by a man and what he was doing to her was feeling mighty good. She couldn't wait to really know what dick felt like. After he verified her wetness, he got a condom and she watched him roll it on. This was it; she was going to have sex. She lay there and closed her eyes tight and waited for him to enter her virgin walls.

Miles took it slow, not knowing she was a virgin, but wondered why he was having a difficult time getting it in. Even though she was good and wet, it slid in and popped out quickly, and it burned like hell to her. He grabbed his dick and held it as he reentered, and she allowed him to go all the way, even though it wasn't a pleasant feeling.

"Ouch, ooh, aw," she said because it burned.

"Are you okay?" he asked trying to figure it out. Juliana did have some tight, good stuff, but she felt new at this moment.

"Yes—it's just been a while—slow, slow, slow," she said, and he was finally inside deep enough to get a steady stroke going. It took a few moments, and then it stopped burning and started to feel good. The only thing that ever entered her body before was a tampon, and now she was really getting some. She held Miles tight as he moaned and worked her love real good.

"Oh, Jules, baby, it's so good. I can't hold it anymore," he said, and she really didn't know what he meant, but when his body jerked, she realized it was over. It was only four or five minutes tops, but it was pure ecstasy for Julia. He rolled over and took a few deep breaths and she lay there smiling. "Are you okay?"

"Yes, I'm lovely," she said smiling at the ceiling.

"What in the hell did you do? Did you go to New York and get that surgery?" he asked, and she was confused.

"What surgery? What are you talking about?"

"When they tighten your body, you know, when they make you like a virgin again," he asked, and she had never heard of such a thing.

"No, Miles, I'd never let anyone go down there to do no surgery," she said looking at him like he was crazy. She knew he didn't know she was a virgin, but to think she had some crazy surgery was absurd.

"I'm just saying, baby, your stuff has always been good, but, damn, tonight it was extra good. I mean, the best I've had in my life," he said getting up to go flush the condom. She was still smiling, and he was ready for round two. He already knew round one was going to be quick, but he was ready to man up and do his thing. "You ready for some more?" he asked licking her nipple.

"Oh, there's more?"

"Baby, you know I'm not a minute-man. That was the one I've been holding for weeks, but now I'm ready," he said, and she was too. He wasn't telling any lies because he rocked her until she couldn't move. Her pussy was so sore she didn't want to be touched at all. They lay in his bed, and the cool air didn't bother their naked bodies as they lay on top of the spread.

He moved next to her and pulled her close. She closed her eyes and smiled to herself. She was in love, and she had no clue how Miles had done that to her in a matter of days. She wanted right then to tell him the truth, but she didn't know what the repercussions would be. She just closed her eyes and enjoyed his body being close to hers. "Are you okay, baby?" he asked tenderly.

"I'm perfect, Miles. Being right here at this very moment with you, I'm perfect," she said. She prayed and asked God to please forgive her for what she had just done with Miles and asked him for strength to resist this man and fell asleep in his arms.

Chapter Twelve

THREE MORE months zoomed by, and Julia was still away from her home and family. She arrived in L.A. almost six months ago, and she missed them so much and was tired of lying to her sisters about why she was still in California because her father was no longer speaking to her. She tried to talk Reg out of it, but he arranged for her apartment at home to be packed up and all her stuff was in storage. Her dad was so upset with her about moving out to L.A. with Juliana he disowned her too and told her that she was no longer welcome in his home even if she did come back.

She kept in touch with her sisters, and since they were holier than thou and didn't follow Juliana's career, they would have never known that Julia was impersonating Juliana. They didn't listen to secular music, nor did they watch worldly entertainment on television. They didn't have a relationship with Juliana like Julia did, so they had no idea Julia was walking in Juliana's shoes.

They had no idea how she lived or how much she had. Not that they cared, so Julia knew they wouldn't come to her rescue. The only thing she enjoyed in L.A. was singing and being with Miles. She spent every free moment she had with him, and they were at the point in their relationship when they said "I love you" when they got off the phone or departed from each other.

She traveled a little and did a few shows in different cities, and Miles was there right by her side. She had her moments where she wanted to talk to him and tell him the truth, but she'd get a threat or two from Reg to remind her that he was still in charge and expecting her to continue to play the role of her famous sister. He pulled her to the side every so often just to make sure they were on the same page.

She was used to her new lifestyle and carried on the charade, but she still cried at night from time to time, and she had moments where she would get very emotional over Juliana. Since no one but Reg, Buster, and Rocky knew she was a twin, no one wondered where Juliana was so Reg got away with murder.

Her family was not missing two sisters because they booted Juliana out of their lives when she moved to New York, and they did the same thing to Julia, because they despised her being anywhere near her sinful sister. Julia was just so frustrated with trying to find a way out, she was starting to lose sight of who she really was.

She got used to being called Juliana. If someone were to call her Julia, she wouldn't answer. Everything about Julia was beginning to fade away, and everything about Juliana had taken form. She even slimmed down a little to be able to fit into some of the dresses that Juliana had that were snug on her at first. She began to become busier with work, and she found less and less time to cook and hang out with Trey.

She tried to balance everything, but found herself exhausted always trying to please everyone. She wanted to just yell out loud that she was Julia and not Juliana, but at that point, who would believe her? Reg had taken her purse and identification; she didn't have anyone to vouch for her that she was Juliana's twin and not her.

Although Buster was the most likely to crack, he still collected a keep-quiet check from the music king of L.A. and wasn't willing to risk it by telling the truth. She had no other options. Reg began to make threats about making Trey come up missing because he knew she cared for Miles so much and loved his son. Miles and Trey had become her new family because Reg, Buster, and Rocky were just a bunch of murderers trying not to get caught.

Hell, her personal assistant Summer worked with her side by side and couldn't tell she was an imposter. Rob, her stylist, who did Juliana's hair and makeup for years didn't know she was a fraud, so how was she going to go to the police without them thinking she was crazy? She had nobody and nothing to back up her story, and since she had been living the life of Juliana Valentine for over five months and never came forward, she knew she'd be spending the rest of her life in a padded room if she went public.

Hell, all the threats were not even necessary anymore, and the surveillance and tracking device and the listening box that Reg demanded that she have at all times while his goons watched her every move was totally unnecessary, and she wanted him to give her some privacy. She was at the point where she knew they watched and heard her make love to Miles. Every intimate moment she shared with Miles was violated by the microphone in her purse.

There were a couple of stolen moments when her purse was not in the same room with her and she could have said what she wanted to say, but she was still afraid to open her mouth in fear of Reg making that one phone call to kidnap Trey, hurt one of her sisters, or destroy her family's church.

She was stuck she thought to herself as she held her head down, praying in service that Sunday morning. She was going to be stuck pretending to be her dead sister for the rest of her life she thought and couldn't stop crying. She prayed and prayed and prayed to God to get her out of it, and she didn't understand why He hadn't delivered her yet.

After the morning devotion they sat and Miles was happy he came to service that morning with her. Most of the congregation was celebrities, and it was different from the Southern Baptist church in Georgia.

Her dad would have never allowed a worldly artist to join or become a member of his congregation if they led a lifestyle like Juliana's so she was happy to be able to go and worship God and indulge in the Word without stares, snares, or comments. She was happy that Miles brought Trey, because she knew he needed to learn about God and have some godly guidance in his life. She hoped that that would not be their last visit.

As the pastor stood before the church and delivered the Word, she continued to pray and ask God for a way out. Miles held her hand. He didn't know the tears she cried were for her dead sister. She silently prayed and grabbed a tissue from her purse. When she laid eyes on the listening device that she had been attached to, she wanted to scream, but she held her peace instead.

Julia dried her eyes as the sermon came to a conclusion. The pastor looked over at her and asked her if she would bless the church with a song. She was shocked. She had been going to that church for a little while and she was never asked to sing, so she wondered why the pastor called on her that day, but she got up and headed to the front of the church.

She walked down the aisle and wondered what song she would sing and if she would play or let the pianist play for her. By the time she made it to the front she decided to sing "The Battle Is Not Yours." She walked over to the pianist and told her that is what she was going to sing. Then she walked over to the pastor. He shook her hand and gave her a hug and handed her the microphone.

Julia closed her eyes and asked God to fill her with the Spirit to bless His people with song. The pianist began to play the song, and she opened her mouth and let her spiritual voice flow. She sang that song not only to the church, but also to herself. She was going through so much at that time and she needed to remind herself that no matter what she was going through, God was going to fight her battles and people like Reg were going to be dealt with by God.

She had to remind herself that God was in control of all things that moved, breathed, and lived on this earth and vengeance is not hers, it's His. Whatever the reason for her sister's death or why she was forced into that horrible situation, God allowed her to be there, and she knew in time He would bring her out.

By the time she was finished singing, the church was on their feet, hands held praising God. She held up her hands and told God, "I quit. You are now employed to work it all out for me." Then she walked over to the microphone stand and placed the microphone in the holder.

She made it back to her seat, and Miles was standing and clapping. Her song moved him and woke up his spirit. He put his head down and grabbed her hand when she stood next to him. He silently asked God to get him back to where he needed to be so he could be a man for him, and he was glad he came. Trey was confused and didn't understand what was going on. All he knew is he liked Juliana's song. When they got in the car, she looked over at Miles and smiled and he smiled back at her.

"Jules, I think we are not utilizing your voice to its full potential. What I just heard in that church was not Juliana Valentine, and I want to know how and why you've held back for so long. I can't remember ever hearing you sing like that, and I just don't understand why you don't give that on your albums and songs," he said wondering why she never sang a song with that much energy.

"Well, Miles, singing for the Lord gives me a different feeling than when I do a CD. You know that gospel and R&B and Pop have a different melody and whatnot," she said trying to conceal her identity again. She knew she was supposed to do it light, but the Spirit took over, and she sang like she sang when she was home in her father's church. The way she knew Juliana could have done too if she still had some kind of a relationship with the Most High. Not that Julia was perfect; she was far from it, but she knew how to pray and repent, and she did strive to be perfect.

"Jules, do you realize you are cheating yourself? Your voice is stronger and better than what you've delivered on all of your CDs and rerecording every song is the best idea Reg has ever had. I know we have a deadline, but at least three songs on this CD should be redone, and I have a song that I want to add."

"What, Miles? Reg isn't going to go for that. He's already on us day in and out with getting this project done. I can't go and tell him that we're thinking of rerecording three tracks and adding another. He'll hit the ceiling," she said hoping he'd drop it. She knew she'd have to hear it from Reg for her solo at church, and she didn't want Miles to keep fanning the flame.

"We've recorded more than half of my album, Miles. We can't just walk in and ask Reg to allow us to rerecord again," she said trying to sway him into a different conversation.

"Jules, come on. All you have to do is go in there and stop holding back and give Reg what you got," he said. Suddenly she didn't want to talk about it anymore so she went along with his idea and just hoped she'd get to Reg before Miles did with his idea. She asked Miles to drop her off at home so she could get a few things to come over to his place. He didn't argue, and as soon as he pulled off she called to the guesthouse and had Oscar, another driver, bring the car.

She pulled out her cell phone and called Reg and asked him to meet her at the studio, and he agreed. She figured whomever was listening in on her at church hadn't reported the solo and the conversation in the car with him yet, and she wanted to get to him and explain.

"Listen, Reg, Miles is going to come to you and ask you to rerecord about three tracks," she said nervously.

"Oh really, why is that? . . . The album is almost done. We're ready to work on your first release video," he said leaning back in his chair.

"Because I sang at church this morning, and I sang like I would have at home," she said nervously. "Please don't be mad, Reg, the Spirit hit me, and I-I—," she tried to say.

"Tore the roof off the church," he said finishing her sentence. Although those were not the words she was going to use, he was correct.

"Yes, Reg, and I'm sorry. I started out light, and I just forgot who I was supposed to be," she confessed, and he was quiet. Her hands were shaking. "Reg, I'm so sorry I messed up. I'm trying so hard to keep it together, but I slip sometimes," she said hoping he wouldn't get up and slap her face.

"You know what, Julia, I'm not mad, and when Miles come to me with the idea of rerecording the tracks, I'm going to allow it. Give him what he wants so we can finish this," he said and she thought her ears were playing tricks on her.

"What? Are you serious?" she asked wondering if he was high.

"Yes, I'm serious. It's time for us to introduce your new sound, and this is the perfect time to do it. People will know it's you from your first video release, and your adoring fans are going to be talking about you in salons and at the bus stop, saying how good Juliana's new CD sounds. They, of course, are going to be just as surprised as Miles and I was, so we will get you on every live show and book your tour as soon as possible. That will show that you are stronger, more beautiful, and most of all, at your best.

"You are getting ready to take Juliana Valentine's career to levels she could never have," he said and lit a cigar. Julia was relieved he was not mad, but terrified about the tour idea. She had no idea about tours and concerts, and she was scared to death with that idea.

"Reg, do you actually think I'm ready to go on tour? I don't know a single thing about going on tour. Hell, I'm just getting used to performing in front of the crowds that y'all have booked me for."

"Look, Julia, you will have time to learn all there is to know about tours and shit, okay? You just have to focus on rerecording your tracks and going platinum—hell, triple platinum. You have time to learn all the routines, and your team will get you tour-ready," he said standing. "Now if you don't mind I have to go," he said. Julia suddenly got the courage to ask him a question she wanted to ask him for months.

"Hold on, Reg, I have another question," she said and stood to face him.

"What?" he asked impatiently.

"Why were you messing with Juliana when you have a wife?" He looked at her like, how dare you question me.

"Well, Julia, a few months ago I told you I'll be the only one asking the questions. Now I have to get back to my wife. Weekends belong to my wife, so please, in the future, don't call me on a Sunday unless you're bleeding from the head," he said leaning in close to her and his evilness sent chills down her spine. She stood there and didn't breathe until he was on the other side of the door.

She blinked back the tears and headed to the elevator and while she stood waiting she looked at her sister's beautiful picture hanging on the wall. She walked over to it and touched the glass. She ran her fingers over Juliana's face and wished they had not been born as twins. If they were not twins, Reg would have never been able to get away with murder and she wouldn't be walking around pretending to be someone she was not.

Chapter Thirteen

COME ON, Juliana, we're going to be late," Trey whined.

"I'm coming, little man. I just have to get one more thing," she said as she put the tracking device into her other purse. She was getting ready to go to one of his soccer games, and she knew she was running late. Baseball had ended, and Trey begged Miles to sign him up for soccer, and after Julia agreed to help him get Trey to his games, he gave in and allowed him to sign up. "All set, let's go," she said, and they hurried out the door. Miles was at the studio. She had promised him she'd take Trey so he could get some work done.

After the game, she sat in the stands and waited for Trey to come from the bathroom. It was taking him an awful long time to come out. She stood and looked around the park. The crowd was getting thinner because mostly everyone was gone. She looked around and decided to walk across the field to the public bathroom to see what was keeping him.

"Trey," she yelled from the boy's bathroom entrance, but there was no answer. "Trey, sweetie, are you in there?" she yelled again, and her heart began to race. A man approached so she asked him, "Sir, my little boy went in there, and he hasn't come out and it's been a while. Can you please check to see if he's in one of the stalls," she asked, and he agreed to.

"Ma'am, I'm sorry, there is no one in there," he said, and she almost passed out.

"Trey!" she began to yell and looked around the park. Her heart was beating out of her chest. "Trey, Trey, where are you?" she yelled as loud as she could. She started running up to people and asking them if they had seen a little boy in a blue and white soccer uniform, but no one had seen him. She ran to the car and got Buster, and they both began to look for him. "Trey!" she cried and yelled hysterically.

She knew she had to call Miles, but she had to look around a little longer because no way he could have just vanished. But after thirty minutes of yelling and looking she knew she had to make the call, and as soon as she took her phone out of her purse it rang.

"Hello," she answered with tears falling.

"Did you lose something?" Reg asked.

"Reg, please, this is not funny. Do you have Trey? Do you have my baby?" she asked not thinking.

"Yes, we are over here," he said, and she turned and saw Reg in a black truck. She immediately ran over. She opened the passenger-side door and grabbed Trey and hugged him tightly. He didn't know why she was so upset. He was only with Reg after all.

"Oh my God, Trey, don't you ever do that again! You never ever leave with strangers," she admonished him.

"Reg is not a stranger, Juliana," he said not having any idea what was going on.

"I know baby, but don't ever leave me or your daddy with anyone, even if you know them without telling us okay," she said kneeling down in front of him.

"Okay," he said and noticed her face was wet. "Why are you crying Juliana," he asked and wiped her face.

"I thought I lost you and I was scared," she said telling him the truth.

"Don't cry, I'm right here," he said and she smiled.

"I know baby, Reg just gave Lia a big scare," she said and Trey looked at her funny.

"Who is Lia," he asked confused.

"I'm sorry baby I meant to say Juliana. Why don't you go over there with Buster and we are going to leave in a minute okay," she said and he went over to the limo and she watched Buster put him in the car. "Reg what in the fuck was that for?" she yelled. She never cussed in her life, but Reg had made her so angry she wanted to spit on him.

"'Fuck?' Oh, you're saying fuck now. I guess you are turning into Juliana," he said and smirked.

"Reg, that wasn't funny, okay! Why would you do that to me? I have done everything you've asked me to do, and you pull a stunt like this? Why would you do that?" she cried with anger.

"To let you know that I'm real and I expect you to continue to do what I told you to do. It would be so easy to take Miles, Trey, Janice and Jada—" he said dropping names of all the folks she loved, and she cut him off before he could say her baby sister or dad's name.

"I get it, Reg, and I know the fucking rules!" she cried and slammed the door. She walked over to the limo and she got in and tried not to cry. She was getting tougher by the day, and no devil in hell was going to break her, she said to herself. "Buster, please take us to the studio," she said. Trey could tell she was upset.

"Are you mad at me, Juliana?" he asked taking her hand.

"No, baby, I'm not mad at you."

"I'm sorry. I didn't know it wasn't okay to go with Reg. He told me that you said I could go with him for some ice cream and meet you back at the park, so I went, and I'm sorry if I scared you," he said rubbing the back of her hand.

"It's okay, baby, and I'm not mad, okay? Just promise me that if anyone, even if you know them or have seen them before, tries to take you anywhere, you run, okay, and come get me or your dad, promise?" she said hoping that Reg wouldn't send someone Trey knew to take him. Trey was at the studio a lot and knew mostly everybody.

"Okay, I promise," he said, and she hugged him. "Juliana, can I ask you a question?" he asked nervously.

"Yes, you can ask me anything."

"Well, our team is having a party, and at the party they have a special dance when all the players on the team dance with their moms, and since I don't have a mom, can you please dance with me?" he asked, and Julia was touched. She knew then that she'd never leave Miles or Trey because she was in love with both of them.

"I wouldn't miss it for the world," she said, and she smiled.

"That's awesome," Trey said and pulled his game out of his backpack. He sat back in the seat, and Julia could see Buster looking at them from the rearview mirror. She didn't have to say a word. Her eyes said all that needed to be said, and Buster looked away. She looked out the window and knew that he was her source to freedom, but she had no idea how long it was going to take. She just asked God that it would be before someone else got hurt.

Chapter Fourteen

"COME ON, Jules, what's wrong? You're giving me the wrong notes on verse two. This song is not hard. You did it yesterday," Miles said talking to her while she was in the booth.

"Baby, I'm sorry. I'm just tired, and I can't do this tonight," she said, because she was still heated about what Reg had done earlier that afternoon to Trey. She was tired of impersonating Juliana, and she wanted to tell Miles the truth and find a way to put Reg behind bars for murdering her sister.

"Babe, come on, you have to. We have a deadline and since we rerecorded those tracks we are off schedule, so come on, babe, take five. Drink some water and let your emotions take over and give this song what you got. This song is about needing someone so bad that you love and you have to make them understand with these lyrics. Come on, Jules, I know you can do it. Just one more run," he said, and she took a deep breath. She walked out of the booth and went into the hall where she saw Reg and Lisa coming her way. Immediately she wished she had never gone out.

"So, Jules, I've heard a lot about this so-called new sound of yours," Lisa said smartly.

"And what's it to you?" Julia said with attitude. Lisa couldn't stand her, well, at least she couldn't stand Juliana, and she was never pleasant or nice to her, and she was not going to stand for her evilness that evening.

"Well, Miss Wannabe Beyoncé, this here is my record company, and every talent that is signed to this label is my concern, and if you weren't a gold mine, trust your contract would never be renewed, so you and this new sound *are* my business, so if I ask you a question, don't get smart."

"Well, Mrs. Towers, it's been a pleasure, but I have a song to record," she said and walked away. She hated Reg, and she hated his wife. If it had not been for Reg wanting to cover up his affair, her sister would be alive, she assumed, thinking that her sister probably threatened to go to his wife about their affair. Julia was so emotional and so upset to have lost her twin and her dad and her home and all of her other sisters. She knew this evil murderer wasn't going to ever let her go. She was upset that she was in love with a man that didn't know who she really was, and she hated deceiving Miles and wanted to tell him the truth every day.

She stepped back into the booth and did exactly what Miles told her to do. She put all of her emotions into that song, and she sang that song to her sisters, her daddy, and to Miles and Trey, because she loved them all so deeply and she needed all of them so desperately, especially Juliana. She swore that she could feel her sister alive some days and thought she could feel her crying and in pain.

There were times when she was having a good day, and then the next moment she'd want to cry, and she thought Juliana was out there somewhere crying too. She knew it was an old saying, but she and Juliana use to really share emotions and she could feel her sister's headaches or if Juliana was sad in Cali she would know it. She'd call, and it would be confirmed that something was wrong or vice versa.

"My heart . . . is aching . . . my days . . . ain't the same. My tears . . . keep on falling, and my nights . . . are so lonely. Each day . . . goes by . . . with no words . . . from you. My darling . . . since you've been gone . . . I've been so blue.

"My heart . . . is aching . . . my days . . . ain't the same. My tears . . . keep on falling, and my nights . . . are so lonely. Each day . . . goes by . . . with no words . . . from you. My darling . . . since you've been gone . . . I've been so blue . . . Oh, I'm missing you," she sang until the music faded.

When she finished the song Miles and the other engineers in the studio were speechless. They were in awe because she sang it so beautifully. When Julia opened her eyes she thought she had made a major mistake the way they were staring at her, mouths opened.

"What . . . Do we have to do it again?" she asked in confusion, because she knew she gave it her all. She put all her emotions and feelings into that song, and she was really too sad and exhausted to sing it again.

"No, baby," Miles said talking in the microphone. "That was perfect, that was unbelievable. You, my love, are phenomenal," he said, and she put the headphones down and let out a deep breath.

"Can we go now, Miles? I really need to get out of this place," she said, and he wondered what was bothering her.

"Sure, sure, just give me ten, or fifteen minutes to wrap everything up," he said, and she came out of the booth. She went and sat on the sofa where Trey was sleeping and gently stroked his face. She fought her tears again. By now, she was so tired of crying. She sat there and shut her eyes and reminisced on her life growing up with her family. She thought about Juliana's smile and how she was always too glamorous, and back then, many Southern folks called her "fast."

She remembered eating Juliana's peas, because her momma would not accept the fact that Juliana didn't like the taste of peas. She wished those days were now, and she wished she could bring her sister back, but she knew she couldn't. She smiled when she remember a boy at their school that liked Juliana, and he asked Julia out instead because he didn't know them apart and how Juliana was so mad at her for not telling her until after the dance. She pretended then to be her sister for a boy to like her, and she was now an adult woman doing the exact same thing.

If Miles knew she was Julia and not Juliana, even if he had met her first, she knew he wouldn't adore her like he adored Juliana, she thought. Suddenly Miles tapped her leg.

"Hey, baby, you ready?" he asked with a sweet smile, and Julia wanted to tell him her secret so, so bad, but she kept quiet.

"Yes, let's go," she said getting up, and Miles picked Trey up.

"Wow, this boy is getting super heavy," he said, and they headed for the exit.

"Yes, he's a healthy boy," she said holding the door for him.

"So how was the game?" Miles asked because they didn't mention it when they arrived.

"Well, they lost by one, but Trey is a good sport," she said as they waited for the elevator.

"That is one of my favorite pictures of you," Miles said admiring the same picture that Julia loved and always touched when she was alone.

"Yea, that is one of my favorites too," she replied admiring it and then the doors opened.

"Miles, can I ask you something?" she asked wondering if he loved Juliana before or after she met him.

"Yea, sure," he said looking at her.

"Did you fall in love with me before or after New York?" she asked nervously.

"Wow, that is a question," he said taken off guard. "You want me to be honest?" he asked, and the elevator doors closed.

"Yes, I want you to be honest," she said, and he didn't say anything the entire ride down and finally the doors opened. He walked out of the elevator without answering her question, and she followed. Miles had his SUV, and Buster was right there as usual waiting. "Hey, Buster, do you mind? I'm going to ride with Miles and Trey."

"Sure, no problem. I'll see you at the house," he said and gave her a warm smile.

"All right," she said and walked over to Miles's truck. He was shutting the back door. He walked around and opened the door for her. By then, she was dying to hear his answer. "So?" she said after he started the ignition.

"Jules, come on, baby, why is that important?" he said, trying to avoid answering.

"Because I want to know," she said looking at him.

"Okay," he said and turned the volume down on the radio. "Before you went to New York you were a hard woman to even like. I mean, you were always uptight and angry and pushy, and it was sometimes difficult to be in the same room with you, but I was so attracted to you that I still wanted you. When you went to New York I missed you, I won't lie, but I didn't miss the bitch that was mean to Trey and waiters and drivers and whomever, so to answer your question honestly, I realized that I was in love with you the day you went to Trey's game with me. That's when I fell in love with you, Jules. It's like you are you, but you're not you. You are so calm now, and you treat people like humans.

"I'm no longer afraid to be in a restaurant with you, and Trey talks about you nonstop, so please don't take offense to what I'm about to say," he said and paused. "I was infatuated with the old you, but I am in love with the new you," he said, and she was speechless. He did fall in love with her and not Juliana. He had an opportunity to love Juliana, but he didn't until he met her, and she felt so good and yet horrible at the same time. She was happy because she won him over being her southern self, and Juliana didn't win him over because she lost touch with herself.

"Miles thanks for being honest," she said and wanted to be honest with him, but her purse was listening, and she knew one false move may cause Reg to make one fatal call.

"Hey, that's what love is about, being honest," he said and that statement made her feel so low. She loved him so much, and it was torturing her to not say it.

"Yea, I guess you're right," she said and turned and looked out the window. When they pulled into her circular driveway, Buster pulled in right behind them.

"Will you need the car anymore tonight?" Buster asked before heading to the guesthouse.

"No, Buster, and thank you," she said and touched his arm.

"No problem," he replied and smiled.

"Good night," she said.

"Good night, ma'am," he replied, and she headed toward

the door while Miles got Trey out of the backseat. They put him to bed in the guestroom where he always slept, and they turned in. They made love again, and it was so good that Julia cried as he stoked her steadily. She moaned a sweet sound in his ear as he sucked on her neck. He slid downward and pulled out and sucked on her breast. He kissed her stomach gently and licked his way down to her clit. Julia was still new to the sex game, and her eyes widened when she felt his tongue lick the southern parts of her body. She wanted to say no, but that was so stimulating to her clit she didn't want him to stop. She reached down and rubbed his head, and he pushed her legs further apart.

"Oh, Miles, oh my, Miles, Miles, baby, ooh, Miles," she moaned and her thighs tremble as she had her first southern orgasm. She and Miles had made love a few times, but he had never gone down on her, and she didn't know that an orgasm would feel like that. "Aww, aww, aww," she screamed, and her legs wouldn't stop shaking. Miles came up and went back to her nipples and pushed his dick back inside of her soaking wet body. He grabbed a hold of her trembling thighs and pumped harder and harder, and he groaned as he exploded inside of her. They were no longer using condoms, because Julia gave in and got on the pill.

He collapsed on top of her, and he couldn't resist giving her a deep kiss. She tasted her own juices on his mouth and wasn't bothered by it one bit. "I love you, baby. I love you so much," he said and kissed her again.

"I love you too, baby, I do," she said, and he lay on top of her for a few more moments. He finally rolled over, and she got up to go to the bathroom. She turned on the water at the sink and decided to brush her teeth and gargle before going back to bed. Then she grabbed her robe because she wanted to go and get a drink of water. "Miles, baby, do you want something from the kitchen?" she asked before going down.

"No, baby, I'm good," he said, and then she went downstairs. She opened a bottle of water and her mind went back to the events that just transpired upstairs and she knew she would have to send Buster to the video store to get her an adult movie or two so she could get some pointers in case Miles wanted her to return the favor. She didn't have a clue of how to do that to him. She finished her water, and as she went back upstairs she was surprised to see Trey up.

"Come on, Dad, please, I had a bad dream," Trey whined.

"Trey, you're a man, and you can't sleep in here with us," Miles said, but Trey was scared to go back into the other room by himself.

"Hey, Trey, come on, I'll go in there with you, and I'll stay 'til you fall asleep," Julia said reassuringly taking his hand, and Miles was glad because he was tired, and he wanted to go to sleep. The two of them went back into the guest room, and Julia climbed into bed with Trey. He lay in her arms, and she held him tightly.

"I wish I had a mom," he said.

"I know how you feel, Trey, I lost my momma too."

"You did?" he asked surprised.

"Yes, a few years ago my momma went to heaven," she said.

"Do you remember your momma?"

"Oh yes, my momma was the greatest, and boy, she could cook," Julia said smiling.

"Well, I never knew my momma. She died when I was a baby. Her pictures are pretty, and she could sing just like you. I used to listen to her songs over and over," he said.

"And why did you stop?" she asked.

"I dunno, just wanted to hear her talk to me instead of sing," he said, and it made sense.

"Well, Trey, I'm sorry you didn't get a chance to meet your momma. She had a beautiful voice," Julia said remembering the CD her hairdresser burned a hole in playing so much. She never bought the CD, but knew all the tracks because for two months straight her hairdresser had that CD in the shop and played it over and over.

"Yea, that's what everybody says," he said, and Julia just held him. They were silent for a little while, and then he asked her, "Juliana, can you sing to me?"

"Right now?"

"Yea, maybe it will help me to go to sleep and not have bad dreams," he said, and she smiled. She had no clue what to sing to a ten year old, but she heard her momma's voice singing "Precious Lord," so she sang it softly. Trey fell asleep, and soon she eased out of bed. She left the lamp on just in case. She kissed him and told God that she would be a good mother to him if that was his will and headed back to bed.

Chapter Fifteen

HERE YA go," Julia said to Buster as she placed a full plate of hot cakes, eggs, grits, and sausage in front of him. She was making sure she was extra nice to him so she could win him over and at least learn where they buried her sister's body. She was literally going out of her mind worrying about the whereabouts of Juliana's body. She wondered if they buried her near the house they kept her locked up in or if they just disposed of her body somewhere else. She wanted to drive out to the house and walk through the woods herself to look for the body, but she had no idea where it was.

"Oh my goodness, Miss Juliana, this is delicious. Girl, you sho'nuff can cook," he mumbled between bites. He was on his second serving, and Julia made sure there was more if he wanted thirds.

"Well, I do what I can," she said loading the dishes into the top drawer dishwasher. She loved her sister's kitchen and thought it would have been lovely if she had a kitchen like that back in Georgia.

"Man, you do it well. When you are outta town my stomach gets mad at you," he joked.

"Well, you know Reg, he keeps us working even when we wanna stop; he has his hooks in you and you can't escape," she said implying that Buster may have wanted to not do what he was doing for Reg but was stuck with no choice at this point.

"Yeah, I know," he said putting his head down and raising his eyebrows. He made a slight nod toward the cameras to remind Julia to watch what she said because they were still being watched.

"Well, when you're done, there's more in the warmer, so help yourself if you'd like more. I'm going to go up. I'll be ready in, say, forty-five minutes, and then we can head to the studio," she said, and he nodded. She walked up to Juliana's room and went into her closet and told herself that she wasn't going to get emotional that day. She told herself that she wasn't going to cry, but there were so many memories of Juliana and her home had dozens of pictures of her beautiful smile and looking at them made her happy occasionally, but sad more often. She heard the sound of Juliana's voice talking to her, and she would replay almost every conversation she had with her that she remembered. Listening to Juliana's music was helpful, but she'd look silly tearing up at her so-called own songs.

Miles noticed that from time to time, and he just thought she was thinking of her late aunt that she supposedly had lost, so he'd just give her a comforting smile and remind her that it will be all right. She wanted to tell him that it will not be all right, because she could not have her sister back. She wanted to tell him that Reg was an evil monster who forced her to hide his dirt, and because of that she fell in love with her sister's man. She wanted to tell him that if it weren't for whatever wicked affair and evilness Juliana had going on with Reg she would be alive that day to do her own songs, tours, photo shoots, and interviews.

She never wanted this lifestyle. It was the life of Juliana Valentine, not hers, she thought as she sat on the floor of Juliana's walk-in closet frustrated because she never knew what she wanted to wear. "Why do you have so many clothes, Jules?" she asked out loud and decided she'd go shower first. She got out and after she lotion her skin, she went back to the closet.

"God, give me strength, please, Lord. I can't take this anymore. Please give me the patience that I need to make it out of this madness. I don't want to be here anymore. I wanna go home. I wanna go home, Jesus. I wanna go home," she cried and broke down. She succeeded for a few days without crying, but it was just too stressful. She sobbed on a pretty blouse that she knew she had ruined with her tears.

She was about to get herself together and get in gear because she knew she was going to be late if she didn't get a move on then suddenly there was a tap at the door. She straightened up as best she could and went to the door. Buster stood there.

"Miss Juliana, are you almost ready? We're going to be late, and you know how Reg is," he said and noticed she had been crying again.

"I'm going to be ready in fifteen, Buster, I'm sorry. I'll hurry," she said sadly, and he felt terrible.

"OK, can I get you anything? Do you need a drink?" he asked, and she was glad he did. She hated that she wanted to drink liquor because she never thought she'd be the one to enjoy drinking. That was always forbidden in the Valentine family, but she needed it, and after a while she felt that she wasn't doing things as bad as her daddy instilled in her. Hell, at that point, she was having sex, drinking, and singing secular music, so she'd just have that drink and add that to her repent list.

"Yes, Buster, can you make me an apple martini and go heavy on the tini," she said with a faint smile.

"Sure, I'll be right back; you just hurry," he said and went down the hall to a lounge area that was on that floor. Juliana's house was definitely a house built for entertainment, and no matter what level you were on, you had access to a drink.

After five minutes, Julia had managed to put on a comfortable, fitted dress. She avoided pantyhose and grabbed a cute pair of Chanel sandals and grabbed the matching bag that was on a shelf directly over the shoes. She kept it simple and put on a little diamond pendant necklace with a pair of diamond studs. When she came out of the dressing area, her martini was on the vanity, so she sat and took a gulp and began to apply her makeup.

She got up and called for Buster to fix her another, and when he came in, she swallowed the remainder of the first drink, and then he took the empty glass. She was never a makeup person, and she didn't need it, but she had to keep up the glam. After a quick blend of neutral colors she removed her satin nightcap and brushed through her hair a bit. She was pleased with the way she looked and never thought she could be that sexy and would always say her sisters would die if they could see her done up so fancy.

Even her more toned figure was gorgeous in everything she wore, and she knew if it wasn't for her imitating Juliana, she would have never taken her look to that level. She polished off the rest of her drink and grabbed her handbag, and Buster was at the bottom of the steps waiting for her.

"Are you all set?" he asked.

"Yes, I'm ready," she answered and followed him out to the car. He opened the door, and she slid in. When he got in the car he let the center window down. He drove out of the gate and when they got onto the main street he put his finger over his lips signaling Julia not to say a word. There were no cameras in the car, but it was wired for sound. He held up his cell phone and she slid over to retrieve it.

She looked at the screen, and it was a message as if he had a text or was going to send a text. She read it and thanked God that Buster was not an evil, heartless bastard like Reg and Rocky. It said, I WANNA HELP U BUT U HVE 2 B PATIENT. SHE IS DEAD N I'M SORRY, JUST GIVE ME TIME. I WILL HELP U, and she almost dropped the phone. She sobbed silently because he confirmed her worst nightmare. Reg was a murderer, and she knew she had to do something before he hurt someone else that she loved.

Buster drove slowly, and although they were already thirty minutes late, he took the long route for her to get herself together. By the time she made it to the studio, she was nearly one hour late. She knew Reg was going to bitch, but she didn't care. She fixed her face and mouthed the words "thank you" as Buster helped her from the car.

He walked her to the door, and when she got on the elevator she felt a little better because at least she had the truth, so there were no more maybes in her head. She just had to pray and come up with a way to get Reg without him knowing that she was coming. When the elevator door opened, she was happy to see that Reg wasn't there, and Miles smiled and greeted her with a kiss.

"Hey, baby," he said. "You look beautiful as always," he complimented.

"Thank you and I'm so sorry I'm late," she said apologizing.

"No, actually you are right on time. I ran over with that young new artist that was just signed, and he is really new to this business. He's going to need a lot of work," Miles said walking over to the piano.

"Oh, OK . . . Where's Reg? I thought he'd be here to yell and cuss me out."

"He's at the hospital with Lisa; they had some type of fertility appointment today. You know they are still trying to get pregnant," he said, and she played it off because Julia didn't know that.

"Really? They still trying, huh? For how long now?" she asked curiously. She knew Juliana had been with Reg for at least four years.

"Shit, for about seven or eight years. I heard they have spent top dollar and have tried everything in the U.S. and overseas. There's something wrong with her uterus or something. I say they should just adopt," Miles said.

"Yea, but I can imagine how she feels. I mean, to not be able to have a child would devastate me."

"Since when? Jules, you've never wanted children, so I wonder how you, of all people, would be devastated. You hate kids."

"No, I don't, Miles. I adore kids. Hell, I feel like Trey is mine," she said defensively. "I want kids, and if I ever get out of this life of BS, I want to have two or three, maybe even four," she said, and Miles couldn't believe his ears.

"Jules, this is madness. You used to love this career and singing thing more than anything and to trade the road and fans and glam to be barefoot and pregnant is not the J.V. I knew a few months ago."

"Well, Miles, people change," she said, and he looked at her strangely. "What?—they do," she said, and he was still looking at her like she was a complete stranger. "Why are you looking at me like that?"

"I don't know, Jules. I don't know what happened to you in New York, but I am in love with you so deep, and you are capturing my heart each day that goes by," he said being straight-up from the heart. She was so sweet and loving, and she was the woman he wanted.

"That's why you are a song writer, because you have a way with words," she said turning away. She had fallen for him deeply too and was scared she was going to lose him as soon as he knew the truth.

"No, Jules, I mean that," he said, and her eyes watered again. She was not Jules, and she wished he could say "Julia" or "Lia" to make his love for her real.

"I want to believe you, Miles, it's just . . ." she said and paused. It was on the tip of her tongue to just tell him, but she thought about Trey, her dad, and her sisters. All the people that Reg could get to before she could get to if he heard her utter a word of truth.

"What is it, Jules? Talk to me, baby."

"It's just . . ." she said afraid, but she wanted to tell him. "If I would have been the same Juliana that I was before I went to New York, do you think you would have fallen for me like this? Like you are now? Would you be telling me this?" she asked still trying to see if it was her or Juliana that he loved.

"Well," he said and thought about it before he replied. He took his time before he answered. "To be honest, no," he said just being straight-up. He had thoughts of just leaving Juliana alone so many times, especially when Trey used to be so sad around her. He told himself that she was not worth his son being so unhappy, but still hoped she'd treat him better. "You were horrible to my son; you were a rude bitch and ordered folks around and always yelled and cussed and fussed."

"How did you even like me at all then?" she asked curiously.

"Well, I don't know, and sometimes I did ask myself the same. I mean, you are beautiful, successful, and irresistible, and you had your moments when you would be sweet. Your loving is insane, girl. I was lucky to have the woman I knew every other man under the sun wanted. When you went to New York I missed you. I missed the bitch, I missed the loving, and I missed your lovely scent. When you came back and you were calm, nicer to Trey, and made an honest effort to be sweet to him, that made me more attracted to you.

"When you started to cook and take care of me and Trey by making sure he brushed his teeth, reading him a book, getting us to go to church, and you stopped drinking every five minutes and snapping off on everybody, I fell in love, so to answer your question, pre-New York, no; post-New York, yes. I fell in love with you after you came home, and whatever changes you made were for the better, so when I tell you I love you, I mean I love you, and I want to be with you, and since we are on this subject, I need you to come with me and I'll show you just how serious I am," he said taking her by the hand.

"Miles, we have a song to work on and a deadline," she said reminding him they had work to do.

"I know, and that song can wait. You must come with me right now," he insisted.

"Wait, I have to let Buster know I'm leaving," she said taking out her cell phone.

"That's fine, but you are riding with me," he told her, and she went along with him. He pulled out his phone and made a call, and Julia wondered where the hell he was taking her.

"Hey, Keith, this is Miles. I need to do this today. Is it ready?" he asked and smiled when he got the confirmation. "Great, I'll be there in like thirty minutes, and Juliana is with me," he said, and Julia wondered what was going on.

They pulled in the back of a store, and Julia wondered why they were taking the back entrance and got nervous. Was Miles in on it with Reg and they were ready to kill her too? Miles rang a bell, and her stomach started to turn flips because she began to feel afraid for the first time with Miles.

"Miles, where are we? What is this place, and why are you taking me in through the back?" she asked hoping he'd say something so at least Buster would know what happened to her.

"Relax, baby, you just wait," he said and touched her face gently, and she began to calm down. Miles was a good man and not like Reg, so she relaxed and a beautiful, light skinned, sexy-framed woman opened the door.

"Mr. Miles, how wonderful. I thought you'd be by later," she said letting them in. "Come on in—I take it this is the one and only Juliana Valentine?" she asked happy to actually see her in person.

"Yes, this is her," he said proudly.

"Wow, Ms. Valentine, you are even more gorgeous in person. I absolutely love your music, and I can't wait until your new CD drops," she said complimenting her.

"Thank you," Julia said modestly, and they followed her.

"You two can have a seat here," she instructed, and they sat on the cozy black velvet armless sofa. Julia looked around and still could not figure out where they were. After about five minutes, the woman came out to get them.

"Miles, Mr. Banks will see you two now," she said, and they went into his office.

"Keith, hey, man, what's going on?" he said shaking his hand.

"Miles, it's a pleasure, and you are the phenomenal Juliana Valentine," he said, shaking her hand gently.

"Yea, that's who they say I am," she replied, and the men took it as a joke, but she was dead serious.

"Have a seat, I know you are anxious," he said, and Julia was clueless.

"Yep, I'm ready to do this," Miles stated, and Keith went over to the safe and opened it, retrieving a red ring box.

"Here you are, and I'm glad we finished it because I didn't expect you today," Keith said handing it to him.

"Baby, Keith is a jeweler that moved out here from Chicago about a year ago. I met him out there. His family owns KBanks Jewelers, and he wanted to relocate, so I put him in contact with a few clients out here in L.A., and he opened the first KBanks Jewelers in L.A., and it's doing well. So he told me whenever I needed something exquisite not to hesitate to ask," Miles said, and Julia's heart started to race. Miles could see that she was still a little lost.

"Look, Juliana, it was so good to meet you. I'm going to give you guys some privacy, and you can use my office as long as you need it," Keith said and pulled the door shut behind him.

"Miles, what's going—?" Julia tried to ask.

"Shhh," he said standing. He took a deep breath and went down on one knee, and Julia thought for sure this was going to be her last breath. No way was he about to ask her to marry him.

"Miles, oh, Miles, oh, Miles," was all she could say.

"Jules, you changed and changed my life too. Trey and I adore you, and we would love it if you'd marry us," he said and opened the box, and Julia just shut her eyes. She sat there with her eyes closed, and even though she didn't open them, a tear fell, and then another.

"Jules," he said, and she still wouldn't open her eyes. "Baby, what's wrong? You don't like the ring?" he asked holding eight karats of beauty in his hand.

"I love it, but I feel like if I open my eyes I'll wake up and this dream will be over so I don't want to open my eyes, baby, because if I do, I know you are going to disappear," she said, and he laughed a bit.

"Baby, give me your hand," he said, and she did without opening her eyes. He slid the ring on her finger, and then he pinched her.

"Ouch," she said opening her eyes wondering why he pinched her. "Why'd you pinch me?"

"To show you how real this is. To show you how real I am and that this right here," he said pointing at her finger, "was specially designed for you," he told her. Julia looked at the ring and silently admired it. It was so beautiful, and she knew Miles loved her.

"Oh my, Miles, I can't tell you what I feel. You know I wasn't expecting any of this."

"I know, but you still have not answered my question," he said, and she had forgotten.

"What, what was the question?" she said because she forgot she never said yes.

"Marry me, will you?"

"Oh, of course, baby, yes, fo' sho," she said imitating Trey.

"Yeah, hey, hey," Keith yelled, and he and two others came in with champagne and glasses.

"Oh my God, oh my God," Julia said and thought to herself she didn't have anyone to call first to tell her good news and her smile faded, but everyone continued to celebrate.

"Oh, baby, we got to call Trey," Miles said, and she was smiling because she had at least one somebody to call. Summer and Rob, yes, but she wanted to call her family.

"Trey, she said yes!" Miles yelled in the phone, and Trey wanted to talk to Julia.

"Jules, you said yes, you'll marry us?" he asked excited.

"Yes, I said, yes. Why didn't you tell me that your daddy was planning to ask me to marry him?" she asked because Trey always gave her the heads-up when Miles was planning something special.

"Well, this was a big secret, and I didn't want to ruin the surprise. Were you surprised?"

"Yes, I was very surprised," she said smiling, looking at Miles.

"This is so cool. Wait 'til I tell Gregory. He's not the only one that's going to get a new mom," he said bubbling over with excitement.

"What do you mean? Gregory has a mom," she said remembering meeting his mom at one of their games.

"That was his dad's third wife; now his dad is getting married to his new mom number four," he said, and Julia didn't want Trey to ever be in that situation.

"Oh, okay, sweetie. I got to go because these people are loud, but your dad and I will see you later."

"Okay, and tell my dad that I said he's the man," Trey said proudly, and she smiled.

"OK, I will," she said and hung up. She took the glass from Miles and gave him his phone, and she wished she could call her family with her news.

Chapter Sixteen

HER RINGING phone woke her, and she frowned when she saw that it was Reg. She went into the bathroom and answered to keep from waking Miles.

"What?" she asked irritated.

"What? What do you mean what, and where in the hell are you? The boys said they haven't heard a word from you in hours, and I was a minute away from calling a hit out on your baby sister," he spat, and she didn't care what the boys said.

"Reg, come on. We should be past this. I've done everything you have asked me to, and I know the rules. Miles proposed yesterday, and we spent some time alone. I know to keep my mouth shut."

"You better, Julia, or you will force my hand. Where are you?"

"I'm at Miles's, and why are you calling me this early on a Saturday morning?"

"Listen, I am going to need you to be at this function today at one o'clock," he said now asking her for a personal favor.

"What function? For who and where?" she asked and flushed the toilet.

"I thought we were clear on who asks the questions," he said going back to asshole mode.

"Reg, please, it's seven in the morning, and you're calling me to show up to something last minute so you can at least give me some details on what it is and what it is for," she said holding the phone between her cheek and shoulder so she could wash her hands.

"Okay, it's an adoption agency. Lisa and I are looking into adoption, and this function is for the agency we are considering going with. I promised the director that you'd show to attract more couples to at least get information on adoption because there are so many children that need homes and getting couples in the door isn't easy, but if you are there to sign a few autographs and maybe sing a song or two for the cause it would help," he said sounding like he actually had a heart, and Julia didn't want to do a damn thing for him. He was a murderer and no child deserved to be in his custody she thought, but she knew he wasn't going to take no for an answer.

"Oh, so now I'm doing shit for you and Lisa's infertile ass? I wonder if Juliana would say yes to helping Lisa out since she is such a cold bitch," she spat being honest. She couldn't stand Lisa, mainly because Lisa hated her, well she hated Juliana.

"Well, Juliana may have not, but you, Julia, don't have a choice because we play by my rules. Need I remind you of your family and your precious little Trey? I know you wouldn't want Miles to die in a horrible accident," he said menacingly, and Julia wasn't so cocky anymore. She thought of her loved ones and backed down.

"Okay, okay, Reg, I'll be there, but I really have to be gone by four. Trey has a special event this evening, and I cannot miss it, okay, so I can do it, but by four I gotta be gone," she said, and Reg was okay with that.

"That's cool; that will work, and then you can go back to your pretend family," he said coldly.

"Listen, Reg, Miles and Trey *are* my family, so please stop insinuating that my life with them is pretend. If it weren't for you, I would have never gotten so close to them, and honestly, Reg, that is the only thing that I can applaud you for," she said and had to lower her voice because she was getting loud. "The only reason I have not told Miles the truth is because you are crazy, and I want them safe because I love them, so don't you dare put my relationship with them into your sick fantasy because they are the only real things to me right now," she said, and her eyes welled. She was so sick of Reg having control over her life. She got to a point where she wanted to kill him herself.

"Yeah, whatever, just be at there by one. Buster knows where it is, so I'll see you," he said, basically dismissing what she just said.

"I'll be there, Reg," she said softly and wiped her tears.

"Fine," he said and ended their call. She stood there for a couple moments and cooled off. Then she climbed back into bed and reached over to set her alarm so she would wake up in enough time to get ready for the function that Reg forced her to do. She closed her eyes and before she knew it, it was time to get up. Miles heard the alarm and wondered why it was set on a Saturday.

"Babe, what's up with the alarm?"

"Reg needs me to be somewhere by one," she said getting up.

"Somewhere like where? You know Trey's dance is this evening."

"I know, baby, and I'll only be a few hours. I told Reg I had to be out of there by four," she said and dragged herself to the bathroom. She started the shower, and Miles came in to use the bathroom.

"Well, I'm going with you," he said, and she didn't dispute.

"Okay, that's fine," she replied and tested the water. She pulled off her nightgown and Miles was turned on to see her naked.

"Ooh, how about you let me suck on these babies before you shower?" he said pulling her close to him and kissing her neck. He gently ran his fingers over her nipples, and she knew she didn't have time for sex.

"Baby, no, come on now. You know the car will be here on time, and I don't want to be late. I want to get in and get out."

"And that's all I wanna do right now," he murmured and slid his fingers between her legs, and she wanted him to get in and get out of her body too, but she had to please Reg.

"Baby, I know, and, boy, do I want to give it to you, but we got to get ready, so please," she begged and moved toward the shower.

"Okay, but you know you wrong undressing in front of me like that," he teased.

"Shut up and go into the guest bathroom and shower, please. We have to be on time," she instructed.

"Okay, damn, Reg is always on you to do shit at the last minute," he complained and went on to shower. They arrived on time, and Julia was grateful. After two numbers she sat to sign a few autographs. Everything was going smoothly, and she felt she was making good time. She just had to write fast because it was like folks were calling people on their cell phone just to come see her and not the children. Miles eased in to make sure she was okay.

"Hey, baby, are you good? We got about thirty more minutes so write fast and cut the conversation," he said in her ear.

"I know, Miles," she said between her teeth. Another fan was standing in front of them, and Julia didn't want to be rude to Juliana's fans. "Hey, can you get me a soda?" she asked, and Miles was off. He came back and another long-winded fan was there holding up the line, and he knew he had to move it along.

Chapter Seventeen

"HERE YOU go, Miss Valentine. Keep in mind we have another engagement," he said out loud, and the woman took her autographed photo and moved on. He stepped back and watched the line grow smaller as Julia tried to scribble as fast as she could. He looked and noticed another thing that was totally wrong. She was signing with her right hand, and he knew for a fact the Juliana was left-handed because he used to always tease her about writing funny. He stood there, and his smile faded. He couldn't wait until she was done. "We need to talk," he said grabbing her arm and forcing her into a corner.

"Miles, what's wrong? You're hurting me," she said, and he loosened the grip he had on her arm.

"What the fuck?" he asked looking at her closely.

"What, Miles?" she asked confused.

"This can't be," he said looking at her strangely. "You look . . . I mean, how?" he stuttered. "Who are you?" he finally asked.

"What?" she asked, surprised, and wondered why he asked her that right then.

"You heard me, who in the fuck are you? Juliana is an evil bitch, that drinks heavily, that can't read music, and hates kids and writes with her fucking left hand!" he said with his jaw clenched.

"Miles please," she said softly and her eyes welled. "Not now, baby, not here. I can't . . . not right now. Please trust me," she said, and her hands started to tremble. He could see that she was scared.

"Why not here?" he asked with his temples flaring.

"It's not safe for us, you or Trey, so please don't ask any questions right now. We will talk, I swear. I just love you and Trey too much, and if I do this right now—," she tried to say, and Reg walked up.

"Jules, thank you so much. I knew I could count on you."

"No problem, Reg. You know I'd do anything for you. I know what would happen to me if I told you no," she said trying to make a joke, but the look on her face told Miles to just be quiet.

"Yea, you know who's in control," Reg said and sorta laughed, but Miles didn't.

"Well, Reg, like I said, Trey has a dance, and I really got to go."

"Sure, Lisa and I thank you for doing this on such short notice," he said, and Miles just stood there. Reg wondered what his problem was. "So, Miles take your lovely lady home and let her get ready for your son's dance."

"Yeah," Miles said, and Julia reached for his hand and squeezed it.

"Come on, baby, let's head out."

"Yeah, um, let's go. Oh, and tell your driver he can go. I drove, so I got Juliana," he said, and Reg didn't like that.

"Um, well, I don't need him to drive me, so Jules should ride with him," he insisted.

"Naw, Reg, I got her," Miles said.

"Okay, and thanks again, Juliana. I know you and Lisa are at odds, but you came through for us, and I'll never forget this," he said to Julia and gave her a look. "You guys stay safe now and have fun with Trey," he told her and walked away.

"What in the hell?" Miles asked, and she squeezed his hand firmly.

"Miles, please, I'm begging you, not now."

"Well, at least a name," he asked, and she was honest for the first time.

"Julia," she said. "And when I walk over there to pick up my purse, I'm Juliana. Trust me, please," she said and went over to the table and reached down under it to pick it up. Miles stood in silence with a million and one questions going through his mind, but something inside of him told him to hold his tongue. When they got in the car, she looked at him and shook her head and pointed at her purse. She put her finger over her lips to let him know not to say a word, and he went along with her. They drove in silence, and when she got out at her house to change she stood and waited for him to say something before shutting the door.

"Trey and I will be here by six. Will you be ready?" he asked looking at her like he wanted to say something.

"Yes, I'll be ready. I love you," she said, and he paused for a moment.

"Love you too," he finally said, and she shut the door. Miles drove home and wanted to call her so bad but decided he'd wait. He was anxious to know what was going on, but he knew from the look in Julia's eyes and from the way things had been the last few months that this had to be something serious. He made it back to his place, and he and Trey dressed and returned to Juliana's house on time. Julia looked beautiful when she got in, and he was in love with that person, so he had to know what was going on.

"Wow, Jules, you look pretty," Trey said.

"Thank you, handsome. You look charming yourself," she said, and he blushed.

"Thanks, Jules . . . I can't wait for them to see us dancing," he said excited, and she was too.

"Miles, baby, you are looking good," Julia said, and he didn't say anything. "Hey, baby, come on now, you have to act normal. We don't want anyone to know that you are jealous because Trey and I have a special dance tonight. If you don't act normal, they will know," she said pointing at her purse.

"Okay, okay," he said trying to go with the flow. "Maybe I'm a lil jealous, okay, but I'm going to act natural as I can. Don't want anyone to think for one moment that I'm jealous of my own son," he said knowing there had to be a listening device in her purse. Julia reached over and squeezed his hand again. She looked at him with earnest eyes, so he decided to trust her until she was able to tell him the real deal.

When they got home, Miles put Trey to bed and came out to rejoin Julia in the living room. "Hey, do you want me to run you a bath?" he asked after she handed him a pad with what to say on it. It read, "Offer to run me a bath to give me a moment to write down all I have to say. After my twenty-minute bath, you say you're going to shower. We exchange a little conversation, and then we turn in, and I will answer all your questions on paper," it said, and he did exactly what she said.

After her pretend bath and his pretend shower, they sat in the bed fully clothed and wrote notes. The first question was the obvious: Where is Juliana? When he read the word DEAD he held his chest and gasped for air. He blinked backed the tears, and she let hers flow. What happened? Was his next question, and she wrote play by play what went down, and he was outdone. He knew she wasn't lying about being Juliana's twin, and he believed her when she told him that Reg and Juliana were having an affair.

The part that he still had a hard time accepting was Juliana being dead and Reg having something to do with it. It made sense though, because of the way he treated Julia after the so-called trip to New York and how she changed after she got back, but he still had a hard time digesting it.

After four hours of note writing, Julia was exhausted and her hand was aching. He held her in his arms and whispered in her ear that he loved her and he would protect her and for her not to worry. She was so relieved to hear him say that so she turned to him and kissed him. They held each other in silence until she drifted off to sleep. Later, Miles got up and undressed and woke Julia and helped her undress.

He pulled the covers over her and kissed her forehead, and she knew then that he truly loved her. To not kick her out and treat her like a lying imposter showed that he was there for her and he was going to be with her through it all. He went to check on Trey again, even though he knew he was safe, but the incident in the park that Julia told him about prompted him to look in on his son. He went to check the door and alarm one more time before going back to bed. Finally, he slid into bed. It took him a little while, but he finally was able to fall asleep.

Chapter Eighteen

MILES GOT up the next morning and left Julia sleeping. As late as he had fallen asleep he was surprised he was up so early. He went into his home gym and got on the treadmill. He was so confused, angry, and furious, and he had no clue about what to do next. He wanted to go straight to the police, but he knew what Julia said about her family being a phone call away from being harmed so he knew that would not be a good idea just yet. He wanted to get in his car and drive over to Reg's and beat the truth out of him, but he knew again that wasn't an option either.

How was he going to continue to go along with Julia being Juliana and how was he going to be able to act natural was running through his mind. Now that he knew the truth, he was going to find it hard not to call her by her real name, so he told himself he'd stick with Jules because Jules could be a nickname for someone name Julia. After he finished his workout, he went back into his bedroom and couldn't resist giving Julia another soft kiss.

He didn't want to wake her, but they had to get up and get ready for church. He was amazed when Julia wrote that her daddy was a minister too, just like his dad was, and he was surprise to know that she had three more sisters, something Juliana had never shared with him. All the things Julia shared with him the night before he wondered why Juliana never told him those things, but then his mind went back to how she was messing around with Reg. That part did not surprise him one bit.

"Baby, wake up," he said kissing her again.

"Nooooo—please, not yet," she whined.

"Come on, it's after eight, and we have to get ready for church," he said pulling back the covers.

"No, Miles, no, I'm so sleepy. Can we skip today?" she pleaded.

"No. What do you always tell me and Trey, huh?" he said quoting her daddy's words. "Would you like it if God skipped you?" he asked, and she knew he was right.

"Okay, baby, okay, but I'm so sleepy. Fifteen more minutes, please," she asked and pulled the covers back up and he remembered that they did have an exhausting night.

"Okay, listen, I'll go down and start breakfast after my shower, and we can skip this one time, but we are not staying here. We are going to eat, dress, and head up the coast for a couple days to get away," he said and her head popped up.

"The coast? Baby, you know I can't go up the coast," she said looking at him like "you know better," and he winked.

"Why not? You're not working, and you have no appointments, so, I wanna take my fiancée away. You used to love it when we drove out and got a room and relaxed. So since we haven't gone in so long, I say we just do it," he said, and she tried to act natural, like she was supposed to.

"I guess you are right. I did love it when we just got away, and the drive would do us some good."

"That's my girl. Now you sleep in a little longer. I'm gonna shower and head into the kitchen and cook, and this time, Trey can tag along with us."

"Yes, that would be nice," she said, and he headed into the bathroom. Julia lay back down and drifted back to sleep in no time. Miles cooked waffles, eggs, turkey bacon, and grits, just like Julia taught him, and they all sat and ate and Julia felt a great sense of relief. Miles was happy to know that he wasn't crazy and Julia was not Juliana; she was Julia. Someone sweeter, more humble and pleasant to be around. She treated his son like a mother would, and he knew that he was going to have to do something to get things taken care of with Reg so he can marry Julia and not the fake Juliana.

"Are you guys all set?" Miles asked as he fastened his seat belt.

"Yes, we are," Julia said with a smile. "Let me run back inside to make a quick call," she said and winked, and he let her. She called Reg. "Hey, as you know, Miles is taking me up the coast for a couple days."

"Yes, I heard, and you know I don't like it," he expressed.

"Reg, I know, but you want me to act like things are normal, yet you forbid me to do normal things. If I tell him no, he is going to give me a hard time, Reg, and you know I'm not going to tell, Reg. I need this break, okay? Just trust me for once," she pleaded, and Reg gave in. He was sure Julia was too afraid to betray him.

"Okay, do your thang, Julia, and I am going to trust that you love your family enough to keep your fucking mouth shut. I don't have a problem with making any one of your sisters disappear, you hear me?" he said with authority, and Julia wasn't afraid anymore, but she agreed.

"Reg, I know the damn rules, okay? I have accepted this for what it is okay, so trust me. If I haven't told by now, you have nothing to worry about," she said, and Reg really believed she feared him enough to keep her mouth shut.

"Okay, kill the mic and have a good time."

"I can trash it?" she asked.

"No, but you can leave it. As soon as you are back in town, I need to be the first person you call, and if I call your phone you need to pick up," he ordered, and she agreed and hung up. She put the little device on the counter and walked back to the car feeling like she was just freed from prison. She smiled at Miles. They were ready to get out of town and talk. They drove about three hours out of L.A., and although Julia left the listening device in L.A. at Miles's place, she still waited until they were checked into their room before they spoke about anything.

She didn't trust Reg and was afraid he may have had Miles's truck bugged too. She text messaged Reg with the hotel info and told him to call the room if he needed to verify she was telling the truth.

Reg texted her and told her that someone was on standby to slice Jada's throat, and that gave her chills. She assured Reg that she knew he was in charge, and she said she knew better. Satisfied with that, he texted her back telling her to enjoy herself.

"Wow, Julia, my goodness, babe, this is so unreal. I mean, you are the best thing to have happened to me, but Juliana being killed makes me sad and angry. I never would have wanted her dead, and you look exactly like her. I mean, you are the splitting image of her, and I just can't believe it."

"Well, that's how God made us, and since all of this happened, I wish we weren't. God knows I want her back. I have lived with this for months, and now I am just wondering what

Reg's next step is. He pulls his little gun out and flashes it every now and then as a reminder to keep my mouth shut, or he'll show me a recent program from my daddy's church to make sure I know that he has someone in Georgia waiting to make it bad for my family, and I am just so tired, Miles," she cried, and he held her. "I didn't want to go along with him, but I was so scared, Miles, and I didn't know what to do.

"He stuck me in this strange city with nobody, and you were the nicest, most gentle person that honestly cared about Juliana, so I trusted you, and I don't have anyone else right now but you," she cried. "My family won't even talk to me, because they think I'm out here sinning my life away, and I don't have any friends I can talk to back home because my family has turned everyone against me. All I have is you," she sobbed, and he held her close.

"Shhh, Julia, don't cry, baby. It's going to be all right, trust me. I'm going to figure something out, okay? I know you are going through hell right now, but I'm here for you, okay? I'm so sorry for what happened to your sister. As bad as Juliana was, I would have never wanted her dead, and I cared about Juliana, but I didn't love her. Not the way I love you. I fell in love with you, and as tragic as things were for Juliana, I am glad I have been blessed with you. You tell me all the time that God is in control and his ways may not be our ways and he brought you out here for a reason.

"Now I would never for one moment say that Juliana being gone is a good thing because it is awful and horrible, babe, but I'm glad God made a way for us to be together," he said, and she lay on his chest. She cried because she missed Juliana, and she cried because she felt bad for being happy with Miles.

"I know God is in control, Miles, and he knows what he's doing, but it doesn't seem fair that she is dead and gone, and

I'm here with you in love and happy with a man for a change in my life. I love you, Miles, I do, but I'd give you up if it meant having her back," she said being honest, and he understood.

"I know you would, baby, and it is perfectly okay to feel that way," he said holding her. She wept for a little while, and he held her and didn't hold back his tears. He felt for her, and he also grieved for Juliana. He knew Julia was afraid to take Reg on, and he didn't want her too. He knew he was going to have to deal with Reg, and he knew he was going to have to come up with a plan to not tip Reg off on what he was doing.

Julia was too important to him for him to risk losing, so he knew if he could help it she was to never be out of his sight. He told himself that he would never allow Reg a moment alone with Julia again, and if he said the wrong thing in the wrong tone, Miles was going to have to check his ass.

"So, Miles, you are not mad at me for what I did?" she asked.

"At first at the adoption agency I was furious and my mind was gone, trust me, but after we stayed up half the night and you explained it all, I wasn't angry anymore, not at you, at least. I was confused and baffled by it all. I'm not mad, just determined to handle Reg. When I dropped you off, something told me to go to the police, but I knew how important the team's dance was to Trey, and he would have been devastated if I told him that we couldn't go or you were not going with him."

"Yes, I was glad you came back for me, because I thought you wouldn't," she said being honest.

"Well, I love you, and we are going to be all right. We are going to get Reg for what he has done, and we are going to expose him for who he is."

"But how, Miles? It's been ten, more than ten, months, and I don't know how we are going to shut him down 'cause it's been so long. There's no telling where he buried my sister, and the police may not believe us."

"I know, baby, but we are going to have to do something. He just can't get away with murder. You can't continue to be Juliana forever."

"I know, and I just wish I knew why he wanted her dead. I mean, she was his mistress, but to kill her . . ." she said sitting up.

"Maybe she threatened to tell. I don't know what would push him over like that," Miles said and wondered again how Reg could do something so insane.

"I don't know, Miles, but I'm so scared. I am so terrified of him, and you have to promise me that you won't jump the gun and tell him. My family is a phone call away, and I don't want to lose another sister or my dad or Trey," she said shaking.

"Listen, Julia, I'm not going to do anything crazy, okay, so don't worry. We are going to get him in due time. I have to think things through before I do anything drastic. Reg is crazy, and I don't want you to get hurt."

"I just wish I could go back to that night and go to her sooner and maybe things would have turned out differently. I play that scene over and over, and if I hadn't drunk or hadda went in sooner, she'd be here, and now she's gone," she said, and her eyes welled again. "I am glad God spared my life, Miles, but I want her here with me. If I hadda heard her sooner . . .," she cried.

"Shhh, come on, Julia, it's not your fault, so stop replaying that night in your mind. What happened to Juliana was awful, babe, but please don't blame yourself for any of it. Reg is going to get his for what he did, and you and I are going to be together and I'm going to protect you, okay?" he said holding her tight. "I'm going to figure it all out, baby. Don't you worry because I got this," he said and Julia closed her eyes. She believed Miles and was relieved he finally knew her secret.

Chapter Nineteen

A COUPLE days later they got back to L.A. and Julia was surprised to see Reg not angry and bent out of shape for her going off with Miles for a couple days. She nervously shut the door behind her after he called her to come into his office. She sat down, and he had a smile on his face, and that had her confused.

"You wanted to see me, Reg?" she asked nervously.

"Yes, I just wanted to thank you for what you did for me and Lisa on Saturday. I know it was last minute, but I appreciate you coming through for us."

"Did I have a choice?" she asked sharply.

"No, you didn't actually, but I wanted to say thanks anyway. How was your trip up the coast?"

"It was good and relaxing," she said trying not to show how nervous she was.

"Good. I see things are still in play. There are no cops at my door, so I can see you are smart enough to keep your mouth shut, so I've decided to cut you some slack and forget about the portable microphone, but understand if you try any funny shit, I will personally slice your throat," he threatened, and her heart almost stopped. There was no trace of the smile he had when she first sat down and she believed him.

"I understand, Reg; I won't say a word, I promise."

"You better keep your word, because if you cross me and try any funny business, my boys will just have to make a visit to one of your sisters, and trust me, it will not be pleasurable for them," he said getting up and walking over to Julia. He put his hands firmly around her neck, and she was shaking like a leaf. "You fuck with me if you want to and—" he began to say, but there was a knock on the door. He removed his hand and straightened his tie.

"Come in," he said. It was Miles. He'd told Julia that he'd wait five minutes and then he'd come for her, and she was relieved when she heard the knock.

"Hey, Reg, sorry to impose, but we have to finish up this track, and the clock is ticking close to our deadline," he said. He could see the fear on Julia's face, and he automatically knew Reg was terrorizing her again.

"No, man, it's cool. Juliana and I were just wrapping up," he said and moved back to the other side of his desk.

"Okay," he said, and Julia rose slowly and moved toward the door.

"Oh, Jules, we are clear on everything we just discussed, right?" Reg said clipping his cigar.

"Crystal," she replied, and Miles put his arms around her waist. He shut the door with his free hand, and he and Julia moved quickly down the hall. "What took you so long?" she asked.

"We said five minutes," he reminded her.

"Well, those five minutes felt like five hours."

"Are you okay?"

"Yea, I'm okay. I just want this to be over."

"It will be, baby, soon. Trust me," he said, and they got on the elevator and went back to the studio to finish the song they were working on. Miles called his travel agent and had her book him a flight for Trey to go to his grandmother's. He wanted to talk to Juliana's father in person to let him know what was going on, but he couldn't go himself in case one of Reg's people spotted him in Georgia, but he had a plan for that. He didn't want Trey to come up missing during his mission to expose Reg, so to get him out of town was the safest bet.

The next day Julia ran into Lisa at the record company. She mentally prepared herself for the tongue lashing Lisa usually had for her, but was taken by surprise when she said hello and thanks.

"Thanks for coming to the agency and thanks for not keeping my husband's baby," she said, and Julia was confused.

"What, what are you talking about?"

"Come on, Juliana . . . you think I don't know that you were pregnant with Reginald's baby. I've known about the affair, and I'm just happy you did the right thing and got rid of that baby and left my husband alone," she said. Julia immediately knew why Reg murdered her sister. She was pregnant, and Juliana wanted to be with him so much she thought the baby would win him over since Lisa couldn't conceive. It made sense, but it was still not a good enough reason to kill Juliana.

"Look, Lisa, I, I, I," Julia said stuttering. She had no clue what to say.

"No, you look, Juliana. I am not as evil as you think, and I stopped liking you or having any type of respect for you when I found out about you and Reg's little love nest downtown. You used to look me in the eye and fuck my husband like it wasn't anything, and when Reg walked in the door that night angry and throwing things I knew it had something to do with you. The next morning I overheard him on the phone making you an appointment to have an abortion. I confronted him on it, and he promised me then he would end his affair and have the pregnancy terminated. I didn't believe him, but after what he said showed true, I knew that Reg loved me more than he loved you, and for a long time I doubted that. So again, thank you for doing the right thing. Never in a million years would I have expected you to show up for us at the agency, but you did that for us, and I appreciate it."

"Well," Julia said still not knowing what to say. "I am sorry for what I did to you, Lisa. I was wrong for having an affair with your husband, and you have every right to hate me. I would feel the same way if a woman did that to me, so I'm sorry."

"Apology accepted," she said with a faint smile. "This doesn't make us friends, but I'm glad we had this conversation today. Trust me, I am a private person, and this conversation will remain between you and me, and I hope we can move on like this never happened," Lisa said.

"Yea, me too," Julia replied, and Lisa walked away. She grabbed her cell phone to call Miles to tell him about the pregnancy, but his phone was powered off because he was in the booth working with one of the other artists on a new track.

■ ■

"Come on, baby, let's go for a run," Miles said wanting to get out and get some air.

"A run?" she asked because she hated working out, and running was never her thing.

"Yea, it will be good, and we can get some fresh air, and then I'll come back and I'll cook for you."

"A run, Miles . . . you know I don't like to run. The only reason I do work out is because Reg thinks I am a cheeseburger away from being a big girl."

"Come on, babe, we need to get out, get some air," he said trying to get out of her house away from the cameras and surveillance so they could talk.

"Miles, I don't know; maybe we could walk," she suggested.

"Jules, come on, stop acting like you are not in shape and too tired to run. Come on, go running with me."

"Fine, I'll go, but make sure you bring your cell phone, just in case you have to call the paramedics."

"Oh, stop it, baby, you'll be fine," he said, and she got up to go change.

"No way was Juliana pregnant," Miles said when they got down the street.

"Well, Lisa said she knew about the abortion and his and Juliana's affair."

"Maybe she was wrong," he said not believing Juliana was pregnant the way she used to treat Trey and how she was so adamant about them using condoms when they made love. She would never let him touch her without one.

"Miles, the woman thanked me for having an abortion and leaving her two-timing husband alone. I don't think she was lying or would approach me like that if that wasn't the truth. Do you think I'd thank your ex-mistress for leaving you alone and aborting your baby? Especially as bad as she wants to have children," Julia said, slowing down. She was getting out of breath because she wasn't use to running.

"I don't know, would you?" Miles said joking, but Julia didn't find that funny. Her sister was dead over this mess, and she wondered why he killed her when Lisa knew the truth. He didn't have to kill Juliana.

"No, I wouldn't, and it's not funny," she said stopping. She couldn't go any farther. "And if I catch you cheating on me, I'm going to cut that penis of yours off," she said. It shocked Miles that she'd say something like that.

"Wow, baby, I never thought I'd hear you say something like cutting off my man. Juliana may have, but not you."

"Well, we both know now who I am, so don't try me."

"Yes, you are my superstar," he said and put his arms around her.

"I'm no star."

"Oh, you are. Your voice is beautiful, Julia, and when this is all said and done, you should continue to sing."

"I don't know, Miles. Juliana was made for this business, not me," she said putting her head down, because she didn't have the talent that Juliana had. She had to practice one routine for a month before she considered herself to be a dancer, and she still felt silly doing Juliana's routines.

"You know you are just as talented as Juliana was; you just have to get your own style and your own rhythm. You can be just as big and good as Juliana was," he said, but she didn't agree. She knew when the truth comes out she would no longer be in that business.

Chapter Twenty

THINK REALLY hard, baby," Miles told Julia because he was trying to get her to remember anything she could about the day she got to L.A. He was so frustrated with trying to expose Reg for what he did, and he wasn't getting anywhere. He was tired of playing and pretending, and he wanted him and his family safe. He wanted Julia to be able to be herself.

"Well, the day I got here, I went to the spa, but I went in as Juliana that day . . . We ordered takeout, and she went into the restaurant to get it, and I stayed in her car. We went back home and that was it. Only thing I can think of for proof is the airline. They have to have a record of me coming and not returning home."

"So there you go. We have the airline to verify that you came out to L.A., and once we get word to your family and get them in a safe place we go straight to the police. Now we have to get Trey to my moms and then we have to get your family out of Georgia," he said and she still didn't see how they were going to get Reg on those circumstances. She didn't have her ID, nor did she know where her sister's body was, and she had no idea where the house was they kept her when they kidnapped her.

"Okay, Miles, that's where this is going to get complicated because my daddy ain't gonna listen to you, and I know he is not going to believe you."

"Your daddy knows your handwriting, doesn't he?"

"Well, yea, but . . .," she tried to say.

"You are going to write him a letter to tell him what's really going on, and he is going to know that this is for real."

"Miles, you don't know my father," she said nervously.

"Julia, your daddy would not ignore a letter with you telling him that he and his other three daughters are in grave danger. No way wouldn't he believe that his daughter was murdered and you have to write everything in a letter," he said, and she knew that was the only way her daddy would come to L.A.

"Okay," she said, and he went to get some help from the only person he considered to be his friend and whom he could trust that didn't know or associate with Reg.

"Come on in, man. What's so urgent that can't wait?" Keith asked as Miles followed him out to his patio.

"Man, listen, I'm about to lay some heavy shit on you, and you have to promise me that you will have my back and keep this between us."

"Okay," Keith said looking at him strangely, wondering what this visit was about.

After Miles was done telling him everything Keith was floored. "Man, damn—how in the hell?"

"I know, but what I need you to do is fly out to Georgia for me and give Julia's dad this letter. I need you to get them on a plane out of there and put them up in a hotel. I can't go because I don't know who Reg has out there watching them or me. I know this is bizarre, but it's all true, Keith, and I can't trust anyone else. I will front you the cash, and we can go from there."

"Okay, man, I will take care of this for you," he said taking the envelope with the cash and letter in it.

"If that isn't enough, I will get you more, but that should take care of you and your hotel as well. I want everything to be first class. This is the name of her daddy's church, so you will definitely catch him there. If not, Julia has written down his home address and her sisters also, but he should be at the church. Julia says he practically lives there."

"Okay, but what if he doesn't believe me?" he asked, but Miles and Julia thought of that too.

"Look, man, I know that is a possibility, but we still have to try. I'm just praying that this works. The sooner we get her family and Trey to safety, it will be easier to go to the police."

"Okay, well, I'll try to get out by morning," he said, and Miles headed for the door. He went home to get Trey and his nanny to get them on a plane out of L.A. too. He didn't let Julia out of his sight, and the next forty-eight hours were like an eternity for Julia. She wanted Keith to call with good news, but he didn't. He told Miles that when he mentioned Juliana and Julia's name and said he was a friend from L.A., her daddy refused to listen to anything he had to say, even when Keith said his daughter was in a bad situation. He told him to leave. Keith said he didn't argue, but he left Julia's letter with him anyway and told him he'd be in town for a couple more days, and he left his card with his number and the hotel information written down on the back.

Julia was so upset to hear that, but she expected he'd act that way. It didn't surprise her one bit because she knew her daddy was stubborn and wasn't a man of reason. She just kept sending up her prayers to God asking him to open her daddy's old religious eyes to the truth. She cried and paced, and Miles paced, trying to come up with something that didn't set Reg off. He held her and kept reassuring her that everything was going to be all right.

Chapter Twenty-one

THE NEXT day Reg was furious. He had no idea where Julia was, and he drove to her house to wait for her. When she walked in, he was sitting on the sofa, and she jumped.

"Oh, Reg, you scared me," she said when she noticed him sitting on the couch. The last two days she and Miles were in a hotel trying to get away from it all and wait for Keith to call.

"Oh, did I? Are you alone?" he asked getting up, moving closer to her.

"Yes, Miles is at the studio," she said nervously and wished he was there with her.

"What are the fucking rules?" he yelled grabbing her hair.

"Ahhh . . . Reg, please, that's not necessary," she cried, but he wasn't going to let her go. "Please, Reg, please."

"What are the fucking rules?" he yelled again, and she was shaking. "I have to be able to reach you at all times," he said pulling harder.

"Reg, please, please let me go. I know the rules, Reg, but it was last minute, and Miles wanted to do something special for me. I didn't know where he was taking me, Reg, and my phone didn't have any battery life left. I didn't know he was taking me to spend a few days alone, Reg. I didn't know," she cried, and he pushed her head.

"You think I'm fucking stupid, don't you?" he asked getting in her face, and she was terrified.

"No, Reg, no . . . I'm sorry. He doesn't know. I didn't tell him. He doesn't know. Why don't you trust me, Reg? I know the rules. There are no cops, no SWAT, no nothing. If I hadda told him, I'd be with a million police right now; please trust and believe me!" she cried hysterically because she didn't know if he was on to them or not.

"Because you and your sister can't be trusted. That bitch lied to me and tried to ruin everybody's life," he yelled, and Julia was praying that he wouldn't hit her.

"I didn't tell him, Reg, and I tried to tell him that we shouldn't just go away, but Miles didn't want to take no for an answer, and it makes him more suspicious, Reg, when I dispute when he tries to do something like that for me, and every time I tell him I can't go someplace, especially without letting Rocky or Buster know, he ask hundreds of questions, Reg. We are engaged. How can I be normal when I am not allowed to do normal things? I never had a problem before now, and Miles is more suspicious when I put up a fight," she cried, and just then, Miles walked in on them and Reg hoped he didn't hear any of their conversation.

"Reg," he said wondering what he was doing there, but after seeing Julia's face he knew he walked in at the perfect time. "Baby, what's wrong?" he said rushing over to her.

"She's upset because I told her that she is going to have to go out of town for a few days, and she's not happy with me right now," Reg said quickly lying, but Miles already knew that was a lie.

"Go where, and why would that upset you so bad?" Miles asked holding her and wanting to kill Reg. He knew he had to do something about him quick before Reg physically hurt Julia.

"Well, baby, I just don't want to go. Now is not the time. I have my release party coming up, and I have videos scheduled, and I'm overwhelmed, and Reg is always signing me up to do shit he knows I don't want to do or can't do, and I'm tired," she said, and she meant it, and he and Reg knew it.

"It's okay, baby, it's work. I can go with you. We can rearrange some things, and if Reg says you gotta be somewhere, just go and get it over with," Miles suggested trying to go along with the bullshit.

"I know but—" she cried.

"Listen, Jules, don't sweat it, okay? I'll try to get another artist to go, but you know they want you," Reg said getting ready to leave. "I'll let myself out, but if you change your mind, give me a call," he said, and he made his exit. They stood in the kitchen, and Miles held her tight. She sobbed. He knew he couldn't talk in the house, but he had to at least calm her down.

"Baby, shhh, it's not so bad, okay? Reg said you don't have to go," he said continuing to play the role. "I know, baby, I know," he said looking her in the eyes, and she knew she couldn't say what she wanted to say.

"He just drives me crazy, Miles," she said putting her hand on her head. She wanted him locked up and far away from her as soon as possible.

"Soon," he said and hugged her again. His cell phone rang. It was Keith so he had to take it. "Baby, give me a minute," he said and stepped away to take the call.

"Hey, man, what's going on?"

"Miles, her dad called."

"Okay, and what did he say?"

"He says he needs to talk to Julia, so take her to the store and call my phone back. I'll pick her dad up in about twenty minutes so call me when you guys get to the jewelry store," he said, knowing his office would be a safe place for them to talk.

"Miles, who was that?" Julia asked when he returned.

"That was Keith. He got a call from his dealer and the piece we wanted for our wedding set can't be done, but he has another option he wants us to come by and see," he informed her.

"Okay, then let's go," she said, and they left.

The pretty, thin, light skinned woman from before took them back to Keith's office. Keith had called and told her to let them into his office when they arrived. Miles dialed Keith's number, and Julia was so anxious to talk to her daddy she was pacing the floor. Although she didn't carry the microphone anymore she still left her purse in the car.

"Hey, Keith, man, did you get Julia's dad?"

"Yes, he's here."

"Okay, I'm going to put Julia on," he said and handed her the phone.

"Daddy," she said, and her eyes got watery.

"Lia, baby, this is your daddy. What on God's green earth is going on?"

"Daddy, listen to me. Everything in that letter is true, and, Daddy, you and the girls have to go with Keith. He's going to bring you guys out here and get you guys into a safe place."

"Look, Lia, your daddy ain't afraid of man, so get yourself to the police and don't worry about us."

"Daddy, no, okay? Listen to me. He killed her," she sobbed. "He killed Juliana, okay, and she has been gone now, Daddy, since the day I came out here to California. He's a dangerous man, Daddy, with a lot of money, and I can't chance it, so please,

Daddy, go with Keith, okay? Don't argue, and I know you're not afraid, but until we can catch this man you are not safe, and I want you here so I can know every day that you're safe."

"It's true? My daughter is gone?" he said, and he sat down. He didn't know what was going on. He just thought Julia and Juliana were pulling some type of trick to get him out there to make amends with Juliana, and now he really wished it was one of their pranks. "No, Lia, no. What happened?" he asked in disbelief. He hadn't cried since his wife died, but he felt a tear roll down his face.

"Daddy, I can't tell you now. Just get my sisters and don't worry, okay? Keith is going to get you guys to a safe place. This man has been watching the church and Jada at the school and Janice at her job at the library and Jessica at the hospital, so you have to talk to them like in a restaurant or somewhere public, 'cause who knows what Reg is capable of. I get photos every week of you guys and I don't know who is watching you all. Tell them that you guys are taking a family trip that you had planned for months and just get on that plane and we'll explain everything when I see you," she said not knowing that Reg only had one person living in Georgia that he was paying a descent salary just to take photos, visit the church, and grab a program because he didn't want to go to jail.

It wasn't an everyday thing; he just wanted to keep Julia in check, and the only way he could keep her doing what he wanted her to do was by threatening her with her family. He had no intentions on causing them any harm even if Julia would have gone to the police. He didn't have a hit man on hand to do the dirty deed, and he didn't want Juliana dead. He just wanted her to give up the baby. That was a horrible accident, and Reg regretted how he handled the situation. He wished he had gone to the police right away and reported it as an accident, but at the time all he could do is think about saving his ass.

She died that night, and they buried her in the woods not far from the house. Reg was paying top dollar for Buster to keep quiet because Rocky was the one who caused her death so he needed to be protected and Buster was messed up behind it so Reg knew he had to pay for his silence.

Now all they had to do is get Julia's family in a safe place, and Julia prayed that they were not being followed. She still was so afraid of Reg, but was so glad Miles was there to protect her. She was also glad he walked in on them that morning because she thought for sure Reg was going to hit her that time. The look on his face and the anger in his eyes had her terrified, and if Miles hadn't walked in, who knows what would have happened.

"Okay, Lia, we'll see you soon, and I won't tell the girls about Juliana until we get there. I just wish . . .," he said and choked up.

"I know, Daddy. I love you, and I'll see you guys soon," she said and gave the phone back to Miles. Miles went over the arrangements with Keith. Her family would make it to L.A. at nine that evening if they made the flight that was scheduled to leave next, so Miles insisted that they hurry. Julia's hands were shaking, but she had a smile on her face that she was finally going to be near her family.

"So what's next?" she asked nervously.

"Buster . . . I'm meeting him in an hour, and he said he'd take me to the house and show me where Juliana is buried. After that, we go to the police, and hopefully, Reg will be locked up within the next forty-eight hours."

"I hope so, and I am so glad that Buster is coming through for us, Miles. I knew he wasn't evil like that crazy Reg. But I'm just so nervous, baby. I'm scared to stay at the house alone. You know Reg barges in whenever he wants."

"Well, baby, you're going to have to be strong for me, and don't let him corner you. Just play it cool. I'll call you every thirty minutes if I have to, to interrupt him if he starts something."

"I just hope he stays away from the house tonight," she said, and they left. Buster and Miles took off in separate cars and met up at Miles's house to park the limo. Julia was so scared she couldn't stop shaking. She just began to sing and pray. She went to the broom closet and started to clean. The place was spotless, but she had to do something. She was in Juliana's room and was dusting a painting of her beautiful sister, and the painting moved like it would fall. She peeped behind the painting to make sure it was on the hook and noticed a safe, so she removed the picture.

She looked at the safe, and then she keyed in her and Juliana's birthday, and it opened. She didn't know what to expect, but she looked through all of her sister's items and was amazed that she had so many pictures of her and her sisters. When she saw a copy of her momma's obituary she smiled. She sent one to Juliana when her mom passed, but she was puzzled that Juliana had two copies. She wondered if one of her other sisters secretly sent her one too.

She looked through the priceless pieces of jewelry and when she saw her momma's favorite broach she cried. Her mom wore that broach for many years, and she remembered it somehow disappearing around the same time Juliana went to New York. She looked through Juliana's contracts and realized her sister did have a lot going on. No wonder she was tired all the time, because she had to fulfill the contracts Juliana had with makeup, skin care, and clothing companies.

She finally came across a copy of Juliana's will, and her mouth dropped when she saw that Juliana left everything to her and her sisters. She left her estate to Julia, and she left a car to each one of her other sisters. She continued to read on, and she smiled to know that Julia left a piece of her fortune to her daddy. She sat there and sobbed for a few moments and noticed a journal so she picked it up. It was full from the first page to the last of Juliana's thoughts and personal stories.

She got up and took a seat on the bed and began to read. Much was written about how she missed her family and how she wished she wasn't considered an outcast. She expressed how lonely she was and how she stopped believing in God because he took her momma away and turned her daddy against her. She wrote about how selfish she thought God was to bless her with phenomenal talent at the cost of her family. She angrily wrote about having to choose between her career and her family, and she thought God wasn't the God that her daddy taught her he was, because no God would bless you to break you, and it was difficult to choose, and her career didn't mean more than her family, she just wanted them both.

Some of the things she wrote made Julia smile and some things made her cry. She looked through all the pictures and hated that she had to tell her sisters that Juliana was gone. She knew they were never close to her twin like she was, but they loved her too. She kissed a picture of her sister and held her journal tight. "I miss you so much, Jules . . . I miss you, baby, and I wish you were here," she said.

She gathered everything and put it all back into the safe. She then began to snoop in Juliana's room and came across a box in the bottom nightstand drawer that she knew Juliana would want their daddy to see. Soon, she looked at the clock and wondered what was going on with Miles, so she grabbed her cell phone and called him.

Chapter Twenty-two

YEA, BABE," Miles said picking up the phone.

"Hey, how's it going?" Julia whispered standing outside on the terrace of her bedroom. Buster assured her that there were not sound wires outside of the house so if she was outside they never knew what was being said.

"Fine, we are almost there."

"Miles, I'm so nervous . . . what if someone is there? Someone may be there, and if they see you, they're going to call Reg, baby, and I'm terrified in this house. Every moment I think he's going to come through that door or send someone else in here to do to me what they did to my sister," she said nervously, now wishing there was a Plan B.

"Julia, don't worry, okay? . . . Buster says that no one is there because Reg didn't want to involve a lot of people. No one other than him, Reg, and Rocky know she's buried out here, and he tries his best to keep away from that house."

"Miles, I don't know. I'm just so scared, and how do we really know he's going to help us? I mean, Buster seems sincere, but he could be setting us up," she said second-guessing Buster's intentions, even though he gave his word that he would help them.

"Julia, don't worry, baby, just pray. We don't know, my love, but we have no other options right now."

"I know, Miles, but I'm terrified."

"I know, and soon this will be all over. I promise I'm going to make it all right."

"I know, but please be careful, Miles, and if it looks funny, please get out of there. Promise you won't do anything heroic. I need you to make it back for me and Trey."

"I hear you, Lia, and I love you, don't ever forget that," he said feeling a little nervous about what she said, but it was too late to turn back. He had to trust God and hope that Buster was legit.

"I love you too, and you don't ever forget that," she said, and the tears fell. She wanted to get off of this emotional roller coaster. She was tired of crying every other day. She wanted this hellish ride to come to an end.

"Okay, I'll call you soon," he said, and they hung up.

"She thinks I'm setting you guys up, doesn't she?" Buster asked because he could hear Julia when they were talking.

"Well, Buster, you were down with Reg."

"No, I was never down with Reg. I was just a bodyguard that made a bad decision; just to so-call make some extra money. I was scared as hell when Rocky killed Juliana, and I was in a panic and went along with whatever Reg said to save my ass. It was horrible what happened to her, and I hate what Julia has gone through. I mean, to lose your sister over a motherfucker who's just trying to cover up his affair and child and be forced to walk around pretending to be your dead sister is horrible," he said, and Miles knew he wasn't being set up.

"I have to face the music and even if I do time, I have to do the right thing, because this bullshit is bad. I would rather give up now so I can free my mind of the guilt I've been carrying for all of these months. I didn't kill her, but I didn't do anything to prevent it either, and trust—I live with that shit every day. I have to do this not just for Julia, but for me because I can't live with this bullshit hunting me every day and that feeling at any moment the cops gon' come get me anyway, because a powerful, rich man like Reg ain't gon' take no murder rap, and he would send me up the river as quick as a ho giving up the ass," he said, and Miles didn't want to laugh, but he chuckled anyway.

"Hey, take this exit," Buster instructed, and Miles got off. He led him to the house where Julia had been hostage for a couple of months, and Miles felt an eerie feeling come over him.

"Buster, are you sure no one is here?" he asked as they slowed to park.

"Man, Reg wants to keep any and every one away from here, in fear they are going to find something to pin him to the murder. He won't even bring Lisa out here anymore, because this is where he hides his dirt," he said, and they got out. They walked around back. Buster pulled out a ring of keys and unlocked the storm door, and then opened the door to the kitchen.

He went over to the alarm system and keyed in the code, hoping Reg hadn't changed it. When the alarm was deactivated Miles came in, and Buster turned on a lamp in the living room. The furniture was covered with sheets to catch the dust. You could tell that the house had not been occupied in several months.

"Come on, let's get Julia's things, and then we can walk out and I'll show you where he laid Juliana's body," Buster said.

Miles wasn't sure if he could handle that, but he followed Buster up the stairs. They went into one of the bedrooms, and Julia's luggage, a sweater, and her purse sat in a corner. Miles grabbed her purse and opened it just to see if what Julia said was really true, and he gasped for air when he looked at her ID.

He saw her Social Security card that said Julia Samara Valentine and shook his head in disbelief when he saw her photo on the license wearing black-framed glasses, no makeup, and her hair pulled back into a schoolteacher's bun. He found her work ID and smiled when he saw she was a music teacher for her local high school, and he wondered why she never said anything about that. He figured Reg made her resign, because she hadn't been back to Georgia in almost a year. He stuffed her ID and cards back into her purse because they still had a lot of ground to cover.

"Come on, let's put her things in the truck," Miles said and they quickly grabbed her stuff. After putting it in the trunk of his SUV, Miles took a deep breath and followed Buster to Juliana's grave. The sun was almost completely down so Buster turned on the little flashlight that was on his key chain.

"She is like in this area here," he said stopping. "If we go to the police I can bring them back here, and it may take a minute, but they'll find her," Buster said unable to make out the exact spot. It had been some time since it happened, and all the ground looked the same.

"Okay, man, let's go," Miles said, and Buster agreed.

They drove a few miles to the sheriff's office. Miles took a deep breath, and he and Buster got out quickly.

"Evening, gentlemen, what can I do for you?" the officer in uniform said.

"Evening, sir, my name is Miles West, and I want to know who I need to speak to, to report a murder," he said and the deputy looked at him strangely. Their little town had no murders. Miles had to be crazy saying that so loudly.

"Murder?" he said and chuckled. "I think you're in the wrong county talking about murder, son," the officer said to him. The sheriff overheard their conversation and came over.

"I'm sorry, sir, but I'm Sheriff Lynwood, and I just want to make sure I heard you correctly."

"Listen, Sheriff, is there somewhere we could talk, because it seems as if the word 'murder' is a foreign word in this part of town," Miles said hoping he'd let him come back and sit and explain the entire story.

"Sure, sure . . . come on back into my office," he said, and his deputy just laughed because he knew Miles being a black man had to be on some kind of drugs. They hadn't had a murder in their town in decades.

Miles followed Sheriff Lynwood to the back and by the time he finished the sheriff was baffled. "So what you're saying is we got a dead singer up at the Tower's vacation home?" he asked still not believing a word he and Buster were saying.

"Yes, sir, that is exactly what I'm saying, and you have to get somebody up there to find her body so you can arrest that man."

"But you said she was killed in L.A.," he said going back to the story they told him.

"Yes, sir, she was, but Reg buried her out here," Buster repeated.

"Well, I'm gonna have to alert LAPD," he said thinking they were feeding him some bullshit.

"Okay, then do what you gotta do," Miles said, and the sheriff decided to challenge their story. He called the next county over and asked for some help with a search party. Since the town was small he called the town judge who happened to be his brother and got a search warrant. Two hours later they were there with hound dogs, and not even two hours after that they recovered what was left of the body of Juliana Tamara Valentine.

"Well, boys, your story turned out to be true and her remains are not recognizable, so it will do you no good to identify the body. Of course, we could have the coroner take a look at her and maybe if we can match her dental records that will speed up the process for ya."

"Listen, we don't have that kind of time. My fiancée and my son could be hurt by this man if he knew what was going down right now. Please, we got to get him off the street," Miles explained.

"Well, I can contact LAPD, explain that we found the remains on his property and we have two credible witnesses—your fiancée and Mr. Gordon here, he said referring to Buster. That will get him arrested on murder charges. However, he will make bail until the body is identified as one Juliana Valentine and wait for his trial. I know he is a big shot out in L.A., so you know bail is going to be easy for him to make. We ship her body back to L.A. and once she's identified as the victim, the state will take it from there," he said, and Miles just nodded his head in agreement. There was absolutely nothing else he could do in the meantime but keep Julia safe. He grabbed his phone and called Julia to fill her in on the details.

Chapter Twenty-three

HELLO," JULIA answered half-asleep.

"Baby, I'm sorry to wake you."

"No, Miles, it's okay. What's going on?" she asked sitting up in the bed, and he told her the details and said he'd be headed back as soon as the sheriff had all he needed. He assured her that she'd be fine and Reg would be arrested soon. He told her he and Buster would be headed back, but Buster was going to turn himself in and may be taken into custody.

She was sad for Buster, but was happy at the same time. Happy to know that Reg would be behind bars soon and sad that she had to go and tell her sisters that Juliana was gone and had been dead for over ten months. She was so anxious to see them and knew going to see them before Reg got arrested would be dangerous.

Finally, ten hours later, her phone rang. "Miles, baby, thank God. Where are you?"

"Pulling up soon. About ten minutes away from you. I arranged for Juliana's remains to be brought back to L.A. There's a warrant for Reg's arrest, and he should be picked up before sundown."

"No way," she said, relieved and in disbelief.

"Yes, baby, it's true. They have enough to make an arrest. And—don't leave the house because Rocky will be having a visitor too from the boys in blue, and they're going to ask you to go in for questioning. I know it will be tough, Julia, but you are safe now, baby, and just tell them everything you remember. I'll be right there to hold your hand, so don't worry" he said.

"Miles, I want to dance right now, and you just don't know how good I feel. I'm not scared anymore, because you did what you said you would, and I love you for going through this with me and for me."

"Yea, the things we do for love," he said.

"What's going to happen to Buster?" she asked.

"I don't know yet; have to wait and see."

"Okay," she said now with dry eyes. She had no reason to cry.

"I love you," he said, and she smiled.

"I love you too," she said and ended the call. She went to pour herself some wine, and then hit the play button on the stereo. She put it on her sister's last CD and didn't cry over her this time. She opened the French doors off of the game room, and Miles walked in to join her shortly after. They sat in silence and held hands until the police arrived. She buzzed the gate and gladly pointed to the guesthouse where Rocky was.

She then went down to the police station. Now she had her true identification on her to prove that her story was legit. She gave her statements and watched them handcuff Buster and walk him out. "We are going to do everything we can to help him," she said knowing Buster was sorry and she had already forgiven him.

"We will," Miles said and put his hand around her waist. They went to the elevators. Julia was finally free. She smiled as they went down to the ground floor. There were so many reporters milling about and cameras set up that they could hardly make an exit. When Julia saw them take Reg out of a squad car in handcuffs she couldn't help but look at him and smile. They fought their way through the crowd and made it to Miles's SUV, repeating the words "No comment."

"Where to?" he asked as if he didn't know.

"The hotel . . . I'm ready to see my family," she said full of excitement.

Chapter Twenty-four

HER HEART pounded with excitement as the elevator climbed the floors and landed on the floor of the four-bedroom penthouse that Miles set them up in. They had plans to take them back to Juliana's home for the rest of their stay. She just wondered how long it would take to have all of Juliana's funeral arrangements done, because she knew her family would be eager to get back to Georgia.

"Jess," she yelled when the doors opened because she was the first one she saw. She was sitting on the sofa watching the news. Julia did not have to tell them about Juliana's death because the word was out and on every station.

"Lia, oh my God," she yelled and hopped off the sofa. She ran and hugged her so hard and tight.

"Lia!" Jada yelled and ran to her too. She had heard them so she ran in from the kitchen. Janice and their dad were out on the balcony, so Jessica ran to let them know that Julia was there.

"Oh my God, girl, look at you. You are gorgeous . . . L.A. has been good to you. You look just like Jules for real," Janice said.

"Yea, I guess," she said and put her head down and she tried not to sob.

"I know, and I'm sorry," Janice said wishing she had not said what she did. Her daddy was waiting to hug her.

"Daddy, oh, Daddy. I'm so happy to see you," Julia said and hugged his neck so tight. She held on to him and cried in his arms. He took his free hand and removed his glasses to wipe his tears, and Jada took his glasses from his hand. After a few moments of everyone standing still and silently crying, Julia let her daddy's neck go. They were so into their reunion, Julia hadn't introduced Miles yet.

"Whew . . . Lord, I'm so glad y'all are here," Julia said and smiled at Miles. "Daddy, I'd like for you to meet Miles West. This is my fiancé. Miles, this is my daddy, Rev. Julius Valentine, and my sisters Jada, Jessica, and Janice Valentine," she said pointing to each one.

"Nice to meet you," Miles said shaking her dad's hand first, and he hugged each one of the girls.

"Miles," Julius said in a deep tone.

"Yes, sir, Miles West," Miles answered nervously.

"Well, Miles thank you for taking care of my daughter and for bringing me and my family out here and putting us up in this beautiful place. We've been watching the news the last few hours so I thank you, young man, for everything you've done to help this family. I am grateful, and I thank God for you. Coming out to California has never been on my to-do list, son, but I realize now that I should have made this trip a long, long time ago," he said, and Julia didn't want to cry anymore.

"Come on, Daddy, come on, let's sit. It's been so long, and I'm just so happy to see all of you."

"Yea, Daddy, come on, sit down. I'll get you some water," Jessica said and went to the kitchen. Her daddy was torn up and wasn't done talking, but he needed a minute. Jessica came back with his water. He took a swallow and handed her the glass.

"I'm just grateful to God that Lia . . .," he tried to say, but he was too choked up. He hated that his eldest was gone and he never told her that he loved her.

"Come on, Daddy, drink some more water," she said, and he took the glass but didn't drink it. Jessica sat on the arm of the couch and rubbed his shoulders.

"Daddy, it's okay," Jada said, and he just sat in silence. Julia knew how bad her dad felt so she decided to lighten the mood.

"Well, listen, you guys, we got a lot of catching up and rejoicing to do. God knows what he is doing. We just have to rejoice and thank him in all things so we are going to thank God for this day because justice was served, and Juliana and momma wouldn't want us moping. They are probably somewhere in heaven singing and dancing together right now because of this day. We are together again, and yesterday has passed away. And we still have each other."

"That's right," Janice said and smiled.

"And y'all know Jules, if she was here right now," she said standing up, "she'd flip her hair," she said imitating her sister, "and cheer us all up by singing," she said, and Jessica hopped up first.

"Yes, she would," Janice amen'd.

"Yea, my baby was never afraid to perform," Julius said and swallowed hard, and the girls knew that he was hurting deeply for his daughter. "I remember the last song she song at the church before she got on that bus," Julius said, and they all remembered.

"Yea, it was 'His Eye Is on the Sparrow,'" Janice said, and Julia grabbed her daddy's hand and started to sing it softly for him. By the time she said, "I sing because I'm happy," they all joined in together. Miles was shocked to see that they all could sing. Julius sat in silence and listened to his daughters sing that song softly . . . while he let his tears flow.

By the time they were done, they all sat and cried for Juliana, and Julia knew that they really missed her. They talked for a little about their childhood growing up together, and they shared stories of their late mom and sister that put smiles on their faces.

"Well, listen, it's getting late, so go and get your bags and get ready. We have a car downstairs, and we're going to go to Juliana's house and cook, and oooh, wait until y'all see her house; it's amazing," Julia said, and she realized she was talking about Juliana as if she was still alive. She left her home to her, but she didn't feel comfortable with saying "my" house.

They gathered their things, and Miles and Julia sat on the sofa and waited for them. "Your sisters are talented as well as beautiful," he said holding her hand.

"I know, and they are going to be blown away when they see Juliana's house."

"You should get used to calling it your house until you settle the estate," he suggested.

"I know it's my home now, Miles, but it belonged to Juliana. I only inherited it, and I'm not sure if I'm going to keep it."

"Well, it's your choice," he said, and Jessica and Jada entered the room.

"Come on, Janice, you are always slow," Jada pouted.

"Shut up, girl, I'm coming," Janice, said and they waited for their dad. They loaded up in Keith's SUV, but Julius and Jada rode with Miles and Julia. When Janice saw Keith and how good looking he was, she ran to the front seat of his vehicle. They rode and ooh'd and aah'd at the city. Julia smiled because she was the same way when she first saw L.A., and she knew Jessica and Janice were behind them in Keith's Escalade doing the very same thing.

Chapter Twenty-five

The Funeral

HELLO AND good afternoon to you all. My name is Julia Samara Valentine. I am the second born child to Rev. Julius and Marie Valentine, and I am overjoyed today for a number of reasons. One is I am able to celebrate the home going of my twin sister Juliana Tamara Valentine. Two, I have been blessed to be reunited with my sisters Janice, Jessica, and Jada Valentine, and it is truly a God-given opportunity to be able to reunite with the pillar of our family, Pastor Julius Michael Valentine.

"At first I was going to sing a song for my sister that I wrote for her to wish her farewell, but she has heard that song before. I have sung it a million times, so I've decided to share with everyone the last entry of my sister's journal instead. The reason I chose to do so is because it gave me peace in my heart to know that my sister did not give up on God, even when I thought she did.

"So, people, never try to guess or say where someone goes even if you've watched them do or say things that are not kind. We truly don't know where folks may end up. The scriptures says that the Lord our God will have mercy upon whom He chooses to have mercy on, so it is never our call," she said speaking up for Juliana because she knew in her heart that her righteous family felt that she was doomed to hell because of the life she lived.

"My sister was a strong woman who reached for the stars and landed on the moon. My sister accomplished things that some may not accomplish in ten lifetimes, but she did it because she had the will and the drive to make things happen in her life. A lot of you here may not have kind words to say about Juliana Tamara Valentine, and some may remember her as surly and not so pleasant to be around, but underneath that tough leather exterior, she had a heart of pure gold, and I don't want the churlish image of her to be the last image you carry with you in remembrance of her," she said and turned the pages of her sister's journal to the page she wanted to read. She paused and took a sip of water before she began.

"Dear God, it's me, Juliana . . . you know, Jules. I have a lot to tell you tonight, and I hope you haven't forgotten me. I really need you right now, and I need you to forgive me for everything that I have done since I've been away. My sister and best friend arrived today and I thank you, Father, for her because she has always been there for me. Seeing her today made me realize how much I miss my family and my top priority is to go home and make things right with my daddy and my other three sisters.

"I know they don't agree with my lifestyle, Lord, but you have to help me, Lord, by preparing their hearts to let me back in, and after I make it right with my family, I'm going to tell the truth about my affair with Reg *and be honest with Miles. I am going to apologize to his son for being so mean to him because he didn't deserve that from me. I want Miles to be*

free so he can find true love for himself and that little boy because he is a good man.

"Lord God, I'm so sorry for treating people the way that I've have treated them, so please forgive me. Lord God, now that I have a child in my womb I want to be a new person, for myself, for my family, and for my child. I've made so many mistakes, and I'm sorry. I will never give myself to another man that is not my husband, Lord Jesus, so again, forgive me. I will raise my child to know you, Father, like my parents did for me. You are my Lord and Savior, and I believe in my heart that Jesus died so that I can live, and I give myself back to you on this day, in Jesus' name I pray."

The church was silent. She closed the journal and took another sip of water. "This was a very personal entry, but I read it so you'd remember my sister Juliana Valentine as the reborn and renewed Juliana Valentine. My sister's death was a tragic and horrible accident, and I miss her dearly, and before I turn it over to my daddy we have a medley that my sisters and I put together of our beloved sister," she said, and the lights dimmed and they began to play Brandy, Gladys Knight, Tamia, and Chaka Khan's, "Missing You." They watched the clip until the song ended, and although it was a funeral people applauded. Julia's daddy came with the closing. Juliana's body had decomposed so badly there was no way they could have an open casket.

Easels stood in the sanctuary of beautiful pictures of her, including the one from the record company Julia loved so much. Everyone left the church and went straight to the cemetery and finally laid the remains of Juliana Tamara Valentine to rest.

Chapter Twenty-six

SO, MILES, when is the wedding?" Julius asked him. They were outside on the patio sitting by the pool while Julia and her sisters were in the house cooking. They decided to stay for a few more days after the funeral. They went to the reading of the will earlier that day and after it was made known that Julia inherited the house, she broke the news to them that she was going to stay in California. The house was definitely going to be sold, but she was definitely going to stay until it sold.

She planned to stay at Miles's because she didn't like being in that house all by herself. It was a gorgeous property, and she knew she would miss it, but Miles's place was just as spectacular. There were too many bad memories of the night of the murder, and she only stayed because Reg forced her to stay. Even though she knew Reg wouldn't dare come near her house now, she still got chills thinking of him. Miles had someone to come out and remove all the cameras that Reg installed, and they installed new locks. Julia now had new round-the-clock security, and Miles vowed she'd never be alone until Reg was convicted and behind bars.

His bail was set at three million, but that was easy for the record king, and he was out on bail until the trial, and Miles hired the best of the best to make sure he didn't do any harm to Julia before the trial. Buster's bail was denied because he had a record, but Julia and Miles still offered to pay for his legal fees because Julia grew fond of him and knew he was a victim like she was. He helped her through her hellish experience and was there for her when she needed a shoulder to cry on.

"I'm not sure, Rev. Valentine, with the funeral and all the excitement around here we haven't gotten around to any dates yet."

"Well, if not when, where are you planning to have this ceremony?" Julius asked trying to keep an eye on Janice talking to Keith over on the other side of the pool. He wanted to order her inside to help in the kitchen, but she was a grown woman, and he couldn't continue to treat his daughters like children.

"Well, Rev., we really haven't talked about that either," Miles said nervously.

"Well, I think a wedding in Julia's hometown at her daddy's church would be a great idea. I've always envisioned all of my daughters getting married there," he said, and Miles knew not to object.

"That's a great idea, sir. I'm sure Julia wants it that way too," he replied and took a swallow of his lemonade.

"Well, that's great, son. I'm sure you want it to be soon, so you can finally touch my daughter. I know waiting is almost impossible," he said, and Miles almost choked on his lemonade. "What's the matter, son? You know my baby is still a virgin," he said, and Miles began to sweat. He didn't want to lie to her daddy, but he couldn't just tell him the truth.

"Um . . . um . . . um," he stuttered wishing someone would walk up to save him from that conversation.

"She is *still* a virgin, *right?*" Julius asked, and Miles thought he would pass out.

"Well, um, Rev . . . Valentine," he said stalling, "Lia and I, um . . . we, um . . .," he stuttered not wanting to tell her daddy that he had been hitting it for months.

"Gotcha . . .," her daddy joked, but Miles didn't laugh. "I knew from the moment I saw her that she had become a woman. She walks, talks, and carries herself like a woman in love, and I know she loves you," he said happy to see Janice heading inside. He knew he was going to have to pull Keith to the side too. "You just take care of my baby. Julia is so special, and she loves wholeheartedly, so don't break her heart. I'm a pastor, but I'm still ole school, so don't make me come lookin' for you with my shotgun," he said, and Miles was shocked.

"No, sir, I won't . . . believe that," Miles said blowing out a breath of air.

"What are my favorite men talking about?" Julia asked coming out and joining them.

"Just men-talk," her daddy said.

"Uh-huh, men-talk, huh?" she said and refilled their glasses with lemonade.

"Yep, just some old-school man-talkin'," he said and took a sip of his lemonade. She went back inside and left them alone. When she got back to the kitchen she heard her sisters whispering.

"Hey, what are y'all in here whispering about?" she asked and they got quiet.

"Nothing," Jada said nervously.

"Come on, y'all, what's the big secret?"

"Miles . . . girl, oh my God, he is fine. Does he have any brothers?" Jessica asked, and she and Jada slapped five.

"Well, I don't care about no brothers. Keith is going back to Georgia with me," Janice said, and they laughed.

"Chile, I ain't never seen a man that fine at home," Jessica said.

"I know . . . the only fine brothers in Georgia are the Williams brothers, and Daddy done scared them off so now they all married," Janice said and they were cracking up.

"Well, I'm thinking about staying out here with you, Lia, because, my God, these brothers look good out here, and Daddy won't be here to say, 'Hey, what you doing in my daughter's face, boy? You betta get from 'round here,'" Jessica said mocking her father.

"I know, tell me about it," Jada said.

"Well, Miles is woo, woo, woo, chile," Julia said and opened the oven to check the mac and cheese and then she went over and poured herself a glass of Pinot and her sisters' mouths dropped open.

"Ooooh, Julia Samara Valentine," Jada said coming off the stool, and it was like they were closing in on her. "You drink the devil's juice?"

"It's not the devil's juice, and it's harmless," she said and got three wine glasses. "Just try it. Y'all are all over twenty-one; live a little," she said, and they all giggled. Julia poured them all a little in their glass, and she made them promise to keep their mouths shut. "We can have more when Daddy goes to bed," she said, and her sisters were game. They tasted and frowned, but didn't stop drinking it. They went back to Julia, wanting to know all the details of her new lifestyle.

"Julia Samara, you ain't no virgin no mo', are you?" Jessica boldly asked looking at the grace Julia had in her movements, and they were on top of her.

"Dang, back up and lower your voices. Daddy is right outside," she said whispering. She stirred the greens, and they all stood there looking at her waiting for an answer, and she told them. "Nope, my flower has been plucked," she bragged, and her sisters were outdone, and they squealed.

"Oooh, Lia, you gave up the goodies," Jessica whispered, and they all moved in closer to her.

"Shhh," she said looking past them to make sure no one came in the room. "Yes, I gave up the goodies, and it is so, so, sooo good," she said making faces and fanning her face like she was going to faint. Her sisters were 25, 23, and 21, and they were still virgins.

"Oh my God," Jada, the youngest said getting all excited. They wanted details. "I am moving to L.A. I don't care what Daddy says," she said like she was ruthless.

"Chile, it wasn't L.A., it was him."

"Well, I need a 'him' too and ain't no 'hims' like that at home," Jessica said, and they laughed.

"Tonight, we are going to stay up late, drink, and we want juice, baby; we need details," Janice said. Just then, Miles walked in, and they all got quiet.

"Um, babe, your dad wants to know how much longer. He says he is hungrier than a lion that ain't ate in seven days," Miles said wondering how Julia's family was so country. He wondered why her sisters were just gazing at him, and he suddenly felt funny.

"Tell him in about fifteen minutes," Julia said, and Miles made his exit quickly. They giggled when he left, and Julia blushed.

"Oooh, ain't he fine?" Julia asked and all of her sisters agreed. After they ate they hurried their dad to bed. Then they stayed up drinking wine and giggling half the night. The next day they slept in late and got up after two. Julia had a show that night, and they headed over for wardrobe because they were going to be her backup singers since they were in town.

Her sisters rehearsed with her a couple days before the funeral and as righteous as her daddy was, he was going to attend the show because he didn't want to do Julia the way he did Juliana, and he vowed he'd not make the same mistake twice.

She was doing her first show from her new CD she recorded titled *The Real Me*. Lisa was kind enough to let her release it under her real name. Julia didn't want to sign a contract with Tower records, and Lisa didn't argue nor did she blame her. They agreed on that one CD, and that was it. Now her soon-to-be-ex-husband was out on bail for the murder of Juliana Valentine. Lisa terminated Reginald Brown immediately after he was arrested at her company Tower Records. He wasn't a Tower. It was Lisa's family's company, and that was why he was deathly afraid of Juliana going public with her pregnancy. He knew Lisa would leave him for sure, because she had been trying to conceive over a decade.

They had an awesome show, and Julius was so proud of his daughters that night, and something in his heart told him to let them be who they are and let God do the rest.

Not long after, the DNA results were in, and the DA had enough evidence to get the ball rolling, and Reginald was put on trial. He was charged with manslaughter, kidnapping, fraud, and four other counts that Julia and her family didn't even know existed. At his sentencing, he apologized to Julia and her family and begged the court for mercy, but he was convicted on all counts and there was no chance for parole. Rocky got the same sentence, and for Buster's cooperation and the statements that Julia and Miles gave on his behalf, he got five years' probation. The Valentines knew to forgive Reg, but they hated that Juliana was gone because of him trying to conceal a pregnancy in order to maintain his wealthy lifestyle.

The family continued to grieve, but life moved on and Julia married Miles at her daddy's church. Julia's dad decided then he'd retire and enjoy his family before his time on earth was gone. Juliana left them a substantial amount of money so her daddy, after months of convincing, finally moved out to L.A. because one by one, each of his daughters moved there, so to be closer to his girl that's where he had to be.

Chapter Twenty-seven

FIVE YEARS later Julia and all of her sisters were married. Janice and Keith hit it off, and she was the first one to move to L.A. and the second one to get married. Their music careers were doing well on Miles's independent label MJT West Inc. Every one of them was doing well doing their own thing, and they were all happy. Julia was finally pregnant after two years of trying, and Trey was fifteen. He was excited about the baby.

"Trey, do not miss your curfew. I'm not playing," Julia preached. He had just gotten off restriction for missing curfew.

"Mom, I won't, okay. I'll be back on time, I promise," he said, and he kissed her cheek.

"You betta because if you pull that same stunt you pulled last Friday you are going right back on restriction," she said trying to be stern.

"Ma, I hear you," he said, and she cringed and held her stomach. "Ma, sit down and get off your feet. You have been doing too much. Let Elsa do what you pay her for," he suggested.

"Yeah, well, Elsa won't be here until tomorrow and this mess you made trying to call yo' self-cooking is not gon' sit in my kitchen until morning," she said grabbing her stomach again.

"I know, but you doing too much," he said, and she moaned.

"Aw, aw, aw," she said, and he rushed by her side.

"Ma, you okay?" he asked just as her water broke. "Oh shit," he said, and she looked at him. "I'm sorry, Ma, but what is that?" he asked confused. He had no idea what was happening.

"My water just broke. Call your dad," she said, and he reached into his pocket and got his cell phone. She carefully walked to the broom closet trying to get the mop.

"No, Ma, what are you doing? Sit down," he said taking the mop out of her hand. He was holding the phone under his chin waiting for Miles to pick up.

"Trey . . . um . . . I . . . can't . . . leave that . . . awww," she cried.

"Ma, please sit down," he said in a panic now because Miles didn't answer. He was in the booth and had no idea his phone was ringing. "Dad's not answering," he said nervously.

"Okay . . . okay . . . okay," she said between breaths. "Call Buster. Tell him to bring the car around. Get my purse and my cell so I can keep trying Miles," she instructed, and he did exactly what she said right away.

"Ooh, oh, oh, oh my God, this hurts," she cried because her contractions came on stronger by the minute.

"Ma, are you okay? What should I do?" he asked scared to death. He did not like seeing her in pain, and he didn't know what to do.

"I'm fine, baby, okay, so don't worry. It just hurts a little. Go into your sister's nursery and get her bag. Go into our room and get my packed bag. Call your aunties and tell all of them that Buster is going to take us to the hospital," she said, and now she was sweating.

"Okay, Ma, but you are scaring me right now. You don't look like you're all right," he said and wondered what was taking Buster so long.

"Baby, relax, it's okay. Just call your aunts and ya grandpa and tell them it's time," she said, and he dialed Julius first. Julia kept dialing Miles, but he didn't pick up, so she finally sent him a text message: MILES, BABY, WHEN YOU GET THIS CALL US OKAY. MY WATER BROKE, AND WE ARE ON OUR WAY TO THE HOSPITAL. Buster finally walked in. He helped her out of the chair, and she was hurting bad by then.

"All right, Julia, take it easy. I gotcha," he said.

"I'm okay, Buster. Come on, Trey," she yelled, and he got off the phone with Jada. She told him she'd call Janice and Jessica and they'd meet them at the hospital. By the time they made it to the hospital, Miles still had not called. When he finally got the right note he was looking for he stepped out of the booth.

He saw his phone lighting up, and he looked at the number of missed calls. He almost dropped his phone when he got the text from Trey saying Julia was in labor.

"Um, Bre . . . I gotta go. Lia's in labor," he told an engineer, and he jetted out the door.

Chapter Twenty-eight

JULIANA TAMARA West," Julius said holding his two-day-old granddaughter. "She looks just like you and Jules when y'all were born. I must say God gave me another twin."

"Yea, he did," Julia said agreeing with her daddy. They were waiting for Miles to bring the car around so they could leave the hospital.

"I should have never shut her out of my life. Your daddy was wrong, and I wish that I could hold my baby again and just tell her how sorry I am for disowning her. I did my part as a parent, and she had every right to live the life she wanted to live, and just because of my stubbornness and self-righteous ways I shut her out and your daddy was wrong," he said letting his tears roll down and holding the baby close. After the trial they didn't talk too much about Juliana, unless they reminisced on the good times.

"It's all right, Daddy . . . Jules knew that you loved her, she did, Daddy, and she loved you," Julia said trying to comfort him.

"No, she didn't hear it from me, and I regret it every day of my life. I disowned my baby girl. I can't believe I did that to her," he said trying to retrieve his handkerchief from his pocket so he could wipe his face.

"Come on, Daddy, let me take Jules," she said, and he gave her the baby and got his handkerchief from his pocket and wiped his face. Julia was in a wheelchair although she told the nurse it wasn't necessary. They said it was hospital policy. They waited for a few moments, and Julia wondered what was keeping Miles.

"I know I can't take back what I did to her, but I live with losing Juliana every day. She was my firstborn and even when you guys were babies, Jules was a performer, and I think she learn to sing before she learned to talk. She was never too shy or scared to do anything. She would grab that mic and open her mouth and share what God blessed her with at the drop of a hat," Julius said recalling their childhood. Julia was always shy, Juliana—she was happy to perform for whomever. "I knew a long time ago that she was born to do what she did 'cause she had it in her to dance, sing, and act, and I kicked my baby out of my life, and I miss her so bad," he cried, and Julia felt his pain.

"I miss her too, Daddy, and don't ever feel that Jules didn't know you loved her because she and I talked about you all the time. When we get back, I'ma give you something that I found when we were packing up the mansion. It's something for you, Daddy. You took Juliana's death so hard I didn't want to give it to you before because I didn't want to add to the guilt you were carrying behind Juliana's death, but now I see that you need it to help you with that guilt," she said, and he wondered what it was. He was going to ask, but Miles finally pulled up.

"Are we all set?" he asked and noticed the sad faces. "Hey, what just happened? When I went to get the car everyone was smiling," he said wondering why the long faces. They had a newborn that was as darling as they come, and he was on ten.

"Just thinking and talking about Juliana," Julia said.

"In that case, we should be rejoicing because God has given us another Juliana to love," he said, and Julius smiled. He knew he could not make up for the time lost with Juliana, but he'd definitely not miss out on little Jules's life and whatever she wanted to be he'd love her and let God judge her.

When they got to the house everyone was there to welcome them home. They had a huge banner that said "Welcome Home, LIL JULES" in big pink letters. There was food, music, and drinks, and Lia did not expect to come home to a surprise party for Juliana. They had a great time, and her first day home was an exciting day. Cameras were flashing, and everyone was fussing over her, just like they did Juliana when she was alive. As the crowd lightened up, Julia gave Miles the baby and asked her dad to come with her. He followed her into the study, and then sat on the leather sofa.

"Now these were found when we were packing up Juliana's things," she said and sat next to him. "Over the years, I sent photos of us to Juliana, and she made this scrap book of me and the girls and Momma," she said handing that one to him first. "And this one she made for you," she said putting it on top of the other one. The cover said "My Daddy," and Julius was afraid to even open it, so Julia opened it for him.

The first page had a big 8 x 10 photo of him, and the second page had a typed description of him that Juliana had trimmed with hearts. Julius was shaking so Julia read it to him. "My daddy, God's number-one soldier. *He is mine and my sister's hero. In spite of our different paths, we are one and the same. We both do what we love to do and give 110%. I love to sing and entertain, he loves to sing and deliver God's Word. Two different paths, but two things that drive us both to be the best. I love my daddy for who he is and what he stands for. My daddy is beautiful inside and out. He has always taught me to stand up for what I believe in. I believe God is real, and he made us all to do something, and my gift is a beautiful voice. Although me and my daddy may not see eye to eye on everything, I understand and respect how he sees things. I miss you, Daddy, and I know you miss me. I love you, Daddy, and I know you love me. We may continue to bump heads and disagree, but we will be together someday, on this side or the other side. Either way, I'll still have my daddy, and we will still end up together,"* she read, and he read the bottom out loud.

"My daddy, Rev. Julius Michael Valentine, is my hero and a great man of God . . . I will always love my daddy," he said, and he held his breath. He looked through the rest of the scrap book and smiled at all the old pictures Juliana had of him and her. Pictures that he forgotten about that he knew his late wife was responsible for giving them to her.

"Thank you, Lia, for saving this for me. If you hadda given me this that day I found out she died, I may have lost my mind," he said because it took him a while to stop blaming himself. He had to continuously pray because her death took a huge toll on him.

"You're welcome, and I think you should take this home with you and whenever you question yourself about how Jules felt about you, you open this book up and read it to yourself. Jules was a good person, Daddy. She just went through a faze, and I think it was because we were not physically in her life, but she heard everything you've said over the years, and when I saw Juliana that day I got to California she was so happy. She smiled the entire time that we were together, and those are the memories I relive in my mind now. Her death was hard, but God knows better than we do."

"I know, Lia . . . I know," he said rubbing the book. "You girls and your momma were my precious gifts from God, and I always wanna be there for you girls."

"Well, Daddy, you can be with all of us as much as you'd like," she said with a smile, and Miles walked in.

"Lia, baby, there you are. I've been looking all over for you. Jules is crying her little eyes out, and I can't get her to stop," Miles said, and Julia instantly got up.

"Okay . . . Daddy, you coming?" she asked because he didn't get up.

"In a minute," he said, and she left him alone. Julia went to get the baby from Jessica, but she was still fussing.

"What's wrong, lil Jules? I know you're not hungry," she said checking her diaper, and it didn't need changing.

"I just changed her diaper about five minutes ago," Jada said when she saw Lia checking it. Julia tried rocking her and tried to see if she'd take the binky, but she wouldn't stop crying.

"Okay, okay, baby, Momma . . . gon' take you to your nursery because you're upset," she said, and Julius walked in.

"Let me try," he suggested, and Lia handed the baby to him.

"Okay, go to your grandpa," she said, and when he took her she relaxed. In a matter of seconds, she stopped crying and everyone was amazed. He rocked her in his arm and headed toward her nursery, and Lia followed him. She stood in the doorway and watched him put her down in her crib. "Don't worry, Jules, I'm here for you, and I'll always be here for you, sweetheart," he said tenderly, and the baby didn't make a sound. He stood and watched over her until she drifted off to sleep.

"I guess you're what she needed," Julia told her dad as they walked from the nursery to go back to join the rest of their family.

"Yep, I guess so," he said and put his arm around Julia's shoulder.

NOW YOU WANNA COME BACK 3

Chapter One

DEVON SAT and looked out the window of his condo and wondered how he went from being happily married to Leila to being an asshole to her, to wanting Michelle for the wrong reasons, to not being able to win Leila back after he finally kicked Michelle to the curb. Then marrying Christa and pushing her away because of his deep feelings for Leila, to finally getting over Leila and falling for Janelle, a woman that he had no clue that was married with two kids.

After a month of waiting to hear from Janelle after their final date, he figured she and her husband worked things out and he wanted his happy ending too. Leila was happy with Rayshon, Michelle married another associate at the office and was having her first baby, and Christa recently announced her engagement to Isaiah at Rayshon's birthday bash.

All he had going for himself was a great career and his fourteen-year-old teenager Deja, who was driving him crazy because she wanted to date. She had less than two months before she'd turn fifteen, and she was so in love with some lil guy at her school named West. When Devon finally met the lil pimpled-face lad, he knew why Deja was head over heels in love. He was damn near Devon's height, with long cornrows in his Puerto Rican waves, and had light eyes that looked like Honey Nut Cheerios. He wore colorful braces, and what impressed Devon the most about this young man was he didn't have his pants hanging off his ass. He was an honor roll student in the same talented and gifted classes Deja was in, but his little princess was two months away from being the approved age that he, Leila, and Rayshon decided on for her to date.

He allowed her to hang out with West as long as it was a group event, but Deja would whine constantly because they wouldn't budge on their decision to allow her to date before she turned fifteen. With only two months until May fifteenth, Devon spent his weekends monitoring Deja's whereabouts, hangouts, and activities, instead of dating or looking for a love of his own. He had become so consumed with fatherhood and trying to keep his one and only daughter boyfriend-free, he was letting life pass him by. He went over to his wet bar and fixed a drink while he dialed Leila.

"Hey, Devon."

"Hey, Lei, what's going on?"

"Nothing too much," she said and looked at her watch. Deja should have been home, and she wondered what was keeping her.

"Where's Deja? I called her phone like five times and I keep getting her voice mail. Is she on restriction again?" he asked because Leila would snatch up her phone with the quickness when she got out of line.

"Nope, and I'm wondering where she is because she was supposed to be home by nine, and I am trying to give her the benefit, but she's trying my patience, Devon, and your daughter is going to end up in a cast. I mean, everything is West this and West that, and she thinks I'm going to say it's okay for them to date, and that isn't going to happen."

"I agree, so where the hell is she?"

"She went to the mall with her lil girlfriend Destiny, and I've told her about not being home on time."

"Okay, well, call me back as soon as she gets in. I wanted to know if she wanted to go skating with my boss's daughter tomorrow. Ever since I took Deja to my boss's house for that dinner, his daughter has been asking Cal when she and Deja can hang out again," Devon said and took a sip of his drink.

"I'll ask her, Devon, but if she doesn't walk through that door in the next few minutes, she won't be going skating or any damn where until her birthday."

"I hear you, and tell her that I said she needs to make sure she takes a charger or that extra battery I got her when she's away from the house, because I don't like not being able to get a hold of her," he expressed, and just then, Deja walked in.

"Oh, here she is now. Do you wanna talk to her?" Leila asked.

"Yeah, put her on," Devon said, and Leila handed her the phone.

"Hello, Daddy," Deja said not ready to hear him fuss.

"Hello, my ass. What did I tell you about your phone? I got you an extra battery last month so you wouldn't come at me with this 'Daddy, my phone died' nonsense, so what happened this time?" he asked losing patience with her.

"Dad, I forgot. I was rushing because Destiny's mom was in a rush, and I forgot."

"Okay, forget again, Deja, and I'll forget to give you back your phone."

"Yes, sir," she said, and Devon continued to fuss her ear off for the next five minutes about being responsible. Finally he told her that he would be picking her up the next day to go skating with Ryan, his boss's daughter.

"Awww, Daddy, no . . . please," she pouted. "Eeeewwww! Daddy, please, no—she is *so* lame, and I don't wanna hang out with her."

"First, you are not going to call Ryan names, okay . . .? That is not how we raised you, D.J. She's a nice girl and wants to hang with you, and you're going to be respectful and nice—and act like you wanna hang with her."

"But why, Daddy? She's like—weird," Deja pouted.

"And you are like one second from being grounded *and* without a phone. Your mom told me you were late again, and this is not the first time I've warned you about your phone, so be ready at four. Put your mom back on," he demanded.

"Yes, sir," she said and handed Leila the phone.

"Yeah, Devon?" Leila said.

"Yeah, if she misses curfew again, Leila, put her ass on restriction," Devon said because he could see Deja going off if they didn't nip her attitude in the bud.

"I hear you . . . So what do you have going on tonight? Christa and Isaiah invited us out for drinks at Jay's. Why don't you join us?" Leila asked because she didn't catch the look on Devon's face when Christa and Isaiah announced their engagement.

"Naw, I'm gon' chill around here and get caught up on some work."

"Are you sure, Devon? I mean, you haven't dated since when, that married chick . . . Janelle," Leila mentioned.

"Oh, so you're monitoring my love life now?"

"No, but Ray and I both agree that you should get back out there. I mean, Christa and Isaiah are doing their thing . . . then there's Kennedy and Julian, Cher and Cortez . . . me and Ray, and then Devon. We all agree it's time for you to at least date."

"Wow, thank you, Oprah and Dr. Phil. You and Rayshon need not to worry about my love life, okay? I have work and a hormonal teen that is in love with some pretty boy named West Ortiz to concentrate on. Love is not on my to-do list at the moment," he said, and Rayshon walked in.

"If you say so, Devon," she said and Ray leaned in to kiss her. "Listen, Ray just walked in. Are you sure you don't want to meet us at Jay's?" she asked again.

"Lei, I'm good, and tell Ray not to forget the game on Sunday. Julian went through a lot to score us these tickets, and he better not be late."

"Okay, I'll tell him," Leila said, and they ended their call. Devon went to refill his glass, and then he went to power on his laptop. He did a quick fridge check and there was nothing he wanted to eat or cook, so he called the local Chinese restaurant that he normally ordered from. Then he got to work and the ringing phone made him jump because his condo was so quiet. He okayed the doorman to let the delivery guy up. Within minutes he was ringing his unit door, so Devon hurried to grab some cash from his wallet. He paid, took the bag, and headed to the kitchen.

He grabbed a pair of chopsticks from the kitchen drawer and opened the white carton to his chicken fried rice. It was after three when he finally shut his computer off and headed to bed. He lay there in the dark and wondered if that was it for him. Had he messed up so bad in the past that God decided not to give him another chance at love? He wondered if he did find someone, was it possible for him to love another woman the way he once loved Leila.

He thought back on how he met her in college and how she was just breathtaking. He didn't think of or want anyone else but Leila after just one date with her. All through college they were close, and he thought Leila had the sexiest figure on the planet. Once they got married, Leila was still looking like a dime piece until her mom died. When her mom passed, she became so depressed and her size eight quickly increased to a ten, then a twelve, and then a fourteen, and then a sixteen, and then she was pregnant. As she picked up the weight Devon remembered just being turned off and he wanted to spend less and less time with her.

He didn't want her to come by his office or even attend any office functions because none of his colleagues had an overweight spouse and he became ashamed of her. They all had wives that lived in the gym even after they had kids. He became so embarrassed of Leila that he stopped taking her places and he'd comment on everything she put in her mouth. He still loved her; that never changed. He still wanted to make love to her because her loving was outstanding, but he just hated her physical appearance.

When she got pregnant with Deja, all his brain told him was she was going to be huge, and that's when he gave in to Michelle's advances. Michelle knew he had a wife when she flirted with him, and she also knew that Devon thought she was sexy.

Their affair was like all affairs—exciting, steamy, and full of hardcore sex. He liked having Michelle on his arm when he entered a room because she was gorgeous. She had an hourglass figure that was even slimmer than Leila's when Leila was at her thinnest. Men looked at him with a look of envy when he was out with her, the look he used to get when he was out with Leila before she packed on the pounds. As beautiful as Leila was, even at a size eighteen when she was pregnant with Deja, Devon couldn't see past her weight. She had the same beautiful face, pretty, thick, shoulder-length hair and almond eyes, but her waistline turned him off so bad that he would lash out at her.

He would be so disgusted he'd call her names and make fun of her thinking that would motivate her to do something about it, but it didn't do any good. She'd get more upset and eat more, and then gain more. By the time she was in her second trimester, Devon had already moved out into his own place. Not because he didn't love her; it was because the physical attraction was gone. Being with Michelle was his escape, but he could never love Michelle like he loved Leila. No matter how he tried to stop loving Leila his heart wouldn't allow him to, and Michelle realized it and finally moved on. Erica realized it and moved on. Tammy realized it and moved on. Jackie realized it and moved on and finally Christa realized it and moved on.

All these women he tried to be with but couldn't because his heart was stuck on Leila. Now that he was over Leila and no longer longed to have her back, he wondered if there was someone else out there for him. Someone he'd love . . . more than he loved Leila. "God, I know I have a horrible past, and I hurt a few, but if you allow me just one more chance at love, I'll never do the things that I've done in the past to hurt her. I just want to be loved. If my wife gains weight, loses her teeth, or whatever . . . I'll love her unconditionally," were Devon's last words before he drifted off to sleep.

Chapter Two

"HEY, GIRLY," Leila said and stood.

"Hey, Lei," Christa said. "This is Janiece, Jaiden's mom, and Janelle, Janiece's sister," Christa said introducing them, and they sat.

"Nice to finally meet you," Leila said to them both, but she couldn't help looking at Janelle. She didn't want to stare, but she thought she looked familiar.

"Well, ladies, as you all know, this is my second marriage, and since I had a small wedding before, my wedding is going to be grand this time. Isaiah says he wants to keep it simple, but what the bride wants, the bride gets," Christa said, and then the server approached. They put their drink orders in and got back to wedding planning.

"Well, I never in a million years would have thought I'd be a part of my ex-husband's fiancée's wedding plans," Janiece said and took a sip of the lemon water that was on the table.

"Welcome to my world. I was in your shoes a couple years ago when I helped my ex-husband and Christa plan their wedding," Leila said, and Christa laughed.

"Oooh, that's right. Wow . . . how do I get close to my man's ex-wives is beyond me," Christa joked.

"I hope Isaiah is a keeper," Leila commented.

"He is," Christa said and smiled. She smiled that smile that Janiece was so familiar with because Isaiah used to put the exact same smile on her face.

"Well, Isaiah is a great man, Christa, and I'm so glad you came along when you did and gave him that love that he deserves," Janiece said.

"Yes," Janelle added. "I mean, my God . . . we've had our soap opera of a past," she said, and they all agreed.

"Yes, indeed, and the thing that separates Isaiah from my ex is that he was and is completely over you, Janiece . . . but Devon, I'm afraid, still has a thing for you, Leila," Christa said, and Janelle froze. She looked around, and it clicked. *Christa and Leila* . . . rang in her ears. She looked at Leila and remembered seeing her in the mall. She blinked a million times and wondered if she should say something, but decided not too, and then she went into her purse to retrieve her phone. She sent Janiece a quick text telling her she had something huge to tell her when they get into the car, and Janiece replied, "OKAY."

"Awwww, Christa, come on. We have had this discussion too many times. Devon loved you," Leila said, and when Janiece heard Devon's name again she still didn't think anything of it, but Janelle knew.

"Yeah, whatever," she said, and the waiter returned with their drinks, and then took their food orders. Leila kept staring at Janelle, but still couldn't remember where she knew her face from, so she thought maybe she worked out at one of Rayshon's gyms.

"Whatever, Christa, I'm just happy you and Isaiah are happy, and I know you may not give a damn, but I can't wait 'til Devon finds love. I mean, after our rocky marriage and his flings and his two minutes of marriage to you, I think he's paid for all the crap he has done to me," she said, and Janelle asked out of curiosity.

"So your ex—this Devon guy is still single?" she asked, and then Janiece looked at her. She then picked up on the name Devon, and she couldn't wait to get into the car.

"Yep, he is, and since he had an affair with this married chick . . ." Leila said and then it hit her who Janelle was. "Oh my God," she said and Leila knew at that point that she was the woman she met in the mall. Janelle was Devon's ex-married lover.

"What?" Christa asked, but Leila didn't say anything, because she saw Janelle's wedding ring on her finger and she knew the entire story. Well, Devon's version. She knew that was the Janelle that lied and cheated on her husband with Devon.

"Nothing," Leila said trying to play it off, and Janelle was happy she didn't air her business.

"It's just, I looked at Janelle, because her name is Janelle, and . . . never mind," Leila said and laughed it off. "Any who, as I was saying, my ex-husband Devon is single and as bad as our marriage was, he is a great guy," she said, and Christa nodded before sipping her drink, and Janiece couldn't wait to get in the car.

"Yes, Devon is a great guy. Fine, sexy, smart, and a beast in the bedroom," Christa joked, and Leila and Janelle both secretly agreed but didn't dare comment. "But, Leila, that man had it bad for you," Christa said again.

"And as I have told you a million times, Devon would have not married you if he weren't ready. You are the one who walked out on a great guy," Leila said.

"And then I met Isaiah, so I'm not mad at the whole failed marriage thingy," she said and waved for the waiter for a refill.

"Wow, so you were married to her ex—" Janiece said nodding her head toward Leila, "and now you are marrying my ex?"

"I guess I am the ex-magnet," Christa said, and they all laughed.

"Well, just be happy; it's smooth sailing from here. Isaiah is one of the sweetest men on the planet," Janiece commented.

"Hey, are you sure you're over him?" Leila joked.

"Oh, yes, K.P. is the love of my life, and I truly believe that all things happen for a reason. All the drama and craziness, ups and downs and turnarounds were only to get us all where we are today," she said looking at her sister, because she figured out that Leila and Christa's ex—Devon—was Janelle's affair Devon.

"I know that's real," Janelle said. "My marriage has survived an affair and lies and hurt," she expressed because Christa was the only one at the table unaware that she had an affair with Devon.

"Girl, you don't know the half of what Rayshon and I have made it through. We now have four kids because my husband's ex–fling's mother passed away six months ago. Shon has a crazy-ass momma who Lord knows I pray that stays locked away forever, because that crazy bitch literally tried to kill me," Leila shared.

"Whhhhaaaattt??" Janiece said. "That doesn't top my ex-husband coming back from the dead after I married K.P., a man that he absolutely couldn't stand. Not to mention K.P.'s crazy-ass ex-wife Kimberly tried to get my ass too, but attacked Janelle while she was pregnant with my niece and nephew."

"Damn," Christa said.

"I guess we have all been through it," Janelle added.

"Girl, not just us . . . wait 'til you meet our girlfriends Kennedy and Cherae. We all have stories to tell," Leila added and now needed a refill. Another round of Cosmopolitans was in order for their trips down Memory Drama Lane. They all shared their crazy stories, and by the time they were done, it was two hours and several Cosmos later. One by one they called Rayshon, K.P., Greg, and Isaiah to let them know they were running late. Finally, they got in their cars, and Leila and Janelle both felt bad for Devon.

Chapter Three

LEILA WALKED in and wondered where everybody was. She knew Deja was going to Devon's, but she didn't expect Ray and the kids not to be home. She put everything down on the kitchen island and went for the wine cooler, because as good as the Cosmos from lunch were earlier, they were weak and the buzz had long worn off. She was exhausted from her day of wedding planning with Christa, and she just wanted a drink and to put her feet up. She noticed her message light blinking so she hit the play button and proceeded to open the bottle of Pinot.

"Hi, Mrs. Johnson, this is Alicia Gray . . . Deja's English teacher. I'm calling because you know the school year is ending soon, and Deja is not doing as well as she was last quarter. She didn't pass her last exam, and I want her to pass this class. Can you meet me on Monday at 12:45 so we can chat? She has always been one of my best students, but lately, her mind hasn't been in my classroom," she said, and there was a beep—letting Leila know that there were no more messages.

She looked at her calendar. She was scheduled to meet Christa at the florist on Monday, and she wouldn't be able to make it, so she called Devon. After a couple rings, it went to voice mail so she hung up without leaving a message. As soon as she sat down with her wineglass and put her feet up, the door chimed and they were home. Leila hoped that Rayshon had fed them, because she was in no mood to figure out dinner.

"Hey, baby," Rayshon said and tossed his keys onto the counter.

"Hey, babe, where were you guys?" Leila asked.

"At the mall . . . Shon is growing out of his shoes every five minutes, so I had to get him a pair of sneakers—with that, lil Ray and Rave got a new pair too," he said and went over, leaned in and gave her a quick peck.

"Man, he is growing like a weed. He is only five and taller than Rave," he commented.

"I know, right?" Ray agreed.

"Hey, Deja's teacher called about her grade slipping in her class and wants to meet with me on Monday at 12:45. Do you think you can go for me? I got wedding stuff with Christa," she said.

"Baby, you know Monday's impossible," Rayshon said going for a beer.

"I know—just thought I'd ask. I'm sure Devon can go," she said getting up. "I don't know what's gotten into Deja," she said and went to add more wine to her glass.

"West, that's what," Rayshon said.

"Yes, West. Lord, if I hear that boy's name again."

"It's her first crush or whatever teens are calling it nowadays," Ray said and leaned against the counter.

"I don't know . . . but what I do know is—if she doesn't get her shit together, she won't be dating at fifteen either," Leila said, and the kids came back into the kitchen.

"Mom, can we have a slice of cake?" Lil Ray asked.

"Sure—wait! Did y'all eat dinner?"

"We had Beggar's pizza," Shon said.

"Really?" Leila said giving Rayshon a look.

"Yes, ma'am," Rave confirmed.

"And y'all didn't think to bring me a slice?" she asked going for the cake she baked to give them a slice.

"Dad said you probably ate with Auntie Christa before he ate the last two slices," Li'l Ray said, and Leila looked at Ray and shook her head.

"Y'all talk too much. Didn't I say in the truck not to tell Mommy where we went?" he said playfully putting li'l Ray in a choke hold, and Leila laughed.

"It's cool. I did eat with Auntie Christa, and we had Portillo's . . . nah!" she teased, and the kids sat at the table and Leila gave each of them a slice of Red Velvet cake.

She and Rayshon went back to the sofa, and Devon returned her call. "Hey, Devon," she said when she answered.

"Hey, Lei, what's up? You tried to call me," he said.

"Yeah, it's about your daughter. Her English teacher called and left a message saying that her grade is going down in her class and wants to meet with me on Monday at 12:45, but I can't make it. Can you meet with her to see what's going on?"

"I'll have to check my schedule. I'll e-mail her and see if I can schedule another time if I can't do 12:45."

"Thank you, Devon. This wedding stuff with Christa has me tied up, so I appreciate it."

"No problem," he said and paused. "Is she really going to marry this dude?" Devon asked.

"Ummm, I'm afraid so, Devon. You're not jealous, are you?"

"Naw, I'm just . . . you know, concerned. They've been dating what? Less than a year," he said trying to calculate.

"Maybe a little more than a year, Devon, and keep in mind you didn't date Christa long before you tied the knot with her," she reminded him.

"Yea, whatever," he said ready to end the call. "Listen, I gotta run—Deja and I have dinner reservations."

"Speaking of your daughter . . . snatch up that cell phone and laptop until you speak with Ms. Gray," Leila ordered.

"Already," Devon said agreeing. Leila got off the phone and told Rayshon she was going to head downstairs and work on some things for Christa's wedding. She was downstairs for a while when Ray went down to see when she was going to come up to bed.

"Hey, Lei, how much longer are you going to be?" he asked, and she looked up.

"Oh, baby, I didn't realize how late it was. I was just putting together some centerpiece ideas to show Christa tomorrow," she said and stood back to examine them. "What do you think?" she asked because she had put together four different options.

"Wow, baby, they are all nice," he said admiring her work. "But it's really not up to me; it's up to Christa and what she likes," he said, realizing Leila had a natural flare for what she was doing.

"Yes, that's true," Leila said cleaning up the mess she made putting the arrangements together.

"Baby, you are really good at this. I mean, these look amazing," he said because he was really impressed. Leila did an awesome job putting together Christa's first wedding in a short time. Now she had more time and a bigger budget so she was making sure Christa's wedding was going to be fabulous.

"You really think so, Ray?"

"Yes, and Christa should be paying you for your service. I mean, look at these. I'm sure she's going to have a hard time making a selection," he said, and she stepped back and took another look at her work.

"Wow, Rayshon, you think they are *that* good?"

"Yes, and I also think you have stumbled into your next career," he advised.

"What do you mean?"

"Wedding planning—hell, not just weddings—party planning. I mean—you put together almost every event that we and our close friends have. Let's see, you did Christa's first wedding in what—like six weeks. You did that modeling soirée for Christa's one-year anniversary at her agency. You threw Catrice from the gym a baby shower bash that they are still talking about, and then that party you threw for Devon that he knows is the reason he now occupies that huge corner office—is because of what a hit that party was. My last birthday party and not to mention the party you are planning for Deja's fifteenth, while handling Christa's wedding . . . Leila, this may be what your next move is."

"Wow, baby, you're right. This does come naturally for me, and I must admit I don't feel like it's work. I'm actually enjoying it. Hell, I can admit that I *love* it."

"So you should give it a try, you know? Find an office space, maybe work out of the house for a moment or two 'til you can build your clientele and maybe hire you an assistant," he said, and Leila began to get excited. She started to feel motivated to go forward with it.

"I can do this for a living. I can," she said with excitement.

"Well, the first thing you need to do is take pictures of these centerpieces. Get as many pictures as you can so you can start a portfolio, build you a Web site and—this is going to be great," he said excited too. He grabbed her and held her tight. "I'm so lucky to have you," he said with a smile.

"Are you?" she blushed.

"Yes . . . you are beautiful, smart, and talented, and I'm like the luckiest man on the planet," he said sincerely. "You've stood by my side through the entire ordeal with Karen, and then when Katherine died, you took Shon in without hesitation, and that makes you like the . . . I don't know. I can't think of a word worthy enough to describe who you are and what you mean to me," he expressed.

"'Incredible' is a word."

"You're more than incredible," he said and kissed her deeply. He pulled her close, and then his dick stiffened in his sweats, and Leila felt it. She tilted her head to the side and gave him access to the side of her neck. Her nipples hardened, so she pulled his hand to her breast, and he began to massage them as she moaned softly.

"Are the kids sleeping?" she whispered between breaths.

"I don't know," he said and went back to her lips and pushed his tongue in her mouth and she pulled away.

"Baby, no, not now. You remember what happened the last time," she reminded him, and he didn't want to stop.

"Leila, they are all the way on the third floor; they won't hear us," he assured her pulling her shirt over her head. The last time they were in their master bathroom getting it in good, Rave overheard Leila moaning, and she busted into the bathroom with a face full of tears and hysterical because she thought Ray was hurting her mommy. Leila was on the vanity with her legs wrapped around Rayshon's waist, and he had a hold of her right tit, sucking on her nipple hungrily, and it was too late. Rayven saw everything. It was awful when they realized she saw them, and they scrambled for a towel, robe, or anything they could cover up with. It took them over an hour to explain that they were playing the Mommy and Daddy "fun game," making sure they emphasized that she couldn't play that game until she was a mom and only with her kid's dad. They told her that the Mommy and Daddy "fun game" was a secret game that she can never tell anyone she saw them play.

Leila's nerves were bad for over a month, thinking Rave would tell her teacher, or Christa, or Deja. They were sure she was going to spill it, but after a couple months, it was like all was forgotten.

"Ray, baby, we can't," she protested, but when he took her nipple inside of his wet mouth, she moaned and grabbed the back of his head and held it tight in place. She reached inside of his boxers and began to stroke his erection. It throbbed as she stroked it, and her pussy began to become moist. He undid her jeans, and she helped him to get them down. "Ooooh, baby," she moaned, and he pushed away his sweats, and she held on to his manhood firmly and stoked it as she rubbed the tip against her stomach.

"Come over here," he said, and she followed him over to the laundry table. "Turn around," he instructed, and when she did, he gave her a slight push forward and she grabbed the laundry table, and he slid in from behind. "Mmmm," he hummed and found his rhythm. Leila relaxed, but she focused her ears and eyes on the basement door. She prayed she and Rayshon could get an orgasm in before they heard the words "Ma" or "Dad." Ray started going deeper, and she forgot about the kids and shut her eyes because the more Rayshon pumped, the better the sensation felt to her body.

"Harder, harder, harder," she said softly, and when he heard that, he grabbed a firm hold of her hips. He hit it harder and harder, and their skin began to slap, and Leila wanted to hold his body and put her tongue into his sweet mouth. "Hold on, baby," she said, and he stopped.

"What, what is it, baby?" he panted. He slid out, and she turned to him and wrapped her arms around his neck and began to kiss him. She leaned back onto the laundry table and tried to hoist herself up, but she needed help, and Ray lifted her up into his strong arms like she was as light as a feather. She pulled him closer to her and lifted her legs with an inviting look in her eyes, and he didn't hesitate. He slid back inside of her and stroked her slowly to a quick orgasm. It was so good to release it. She moaned while sucking on his neck as if he didn't have beads of sweat running down. It was salty, but she didn't mind one bit. "You got yours, baby?" he asked.

"Yes yes, yes!" she breathed out, and he wanted to get his.

"So can yo' man get his?" he asked, and she didn't want to move, but she slid down. She went over to the sofa, and he sat down, and she turned her back to him and slid down on him like he liked her to ride him—facing frontwards. Once she slid down on it, it didn't take Rayshon long to cum, because Leila had mastered her technique of riding him that way. He grabbed her breasts firmly and tried to muffle the sounds of his groans in her back, but it was loud enough to wake the dead if they were in the next room. "Baby, damn . . . damn," he expressed, and she fell back on him.

"So what now?" she asked not wanting to climb the steps.

"Sleep," he said.

"I agree," she said and finally got up.

about the author

ANNA BLACK is a native of Chicago, but now resides in Texas with her husband and daughter. *Split Image* is her sixth published fiction novel, and she will soon release her seventh novel, Now You Wanna Come Back 3. She is a GM for a hotel in Groesbeck, Texas and her goal is to become a fulltime author and publisher.

Anna would love to hear from her readers and supporters, so please feel free to contact her at the following:

www.annablack.net

www.annablackreaders@ymail.com

www.twitter.com/AnnBlack72

www.facebook.com/AuthoressAnnaBlack

Made in the USA
San Bernardino, CA
26 October 2013